A REAL ONLINE FANTASY

PARTS 1 & 2

CATE ELLINK

CONTENTS

Acknowledgments   vii

Part 1   1
Part 2   35

BONUS CONTENT
Pain Surfer   59
Control   66
Michaels's Moment   71
About the Author   95
Other Books by Cate Ellink   97

Published by Cate Ellink

Cover Design and Formatting: Paradox Book Covers and Formatting

Part 1 of this story was previously published by Momentum in 2012.

Part 2 has been added and the work has been re-released.

ISBN (mobi) 978-0-6485314-1-8
ISBN (ePub) 978-0-6485314-2-5
ISBN (print) 978-0-6485314-3-2

BLURB

Can an online fantasy ever become real?

When Condamine connects with Esquire in a chat room, neither expect their mutual pleasure and close friendship will become something far more intimate and real. But when the opportunity to meet Esquire in the flesh comes up will Condamine – Caitlyn, in real life – be bold enough to act out her deepest fantasies, or will she hide away from the world behind the comfortable glare of her computer screen?

ACKNOWLEDGMENTS

A book is never a solo journey—well, mine certainly aren't.

Special thanks to -

- Mum and Dad who taught me to love reading and encouraged my imagination.
- Stephan, who believed I could write long before I did. Thank you for reading, challenging me and encouraging me endlessly.
- The Romance Writers of Australia. Without this group of generous, supportive, amazing women, and men, I'd still be thinking *I'd like to write a book one day*.
- My critique partners, Mervet, Judy and Sandra, who've been on the journey from the start.
- Anne Gracie, Bronwyn Jameson and the Romance Intensive workshop that taught me I needed to learn a hell of a lot.
- Anita Joy, Ainslie Paton, Anthea Laurelton, Sheridan Kent, Kaliana Cole, Mel Teshco, Tracey O'Hara, Angela Castle and Jess Dee for reading drafts and giving great suggestions.
- The Hot Down Under girls - Tracie Sommers, Mel Teshco, Kasey Channing,

Kylie Scott, Rhyll Biest, Rhian Cahill, SE Gilchrist, Marianne Theresa, CT Green, Keziah Hill, Shona Husk, Beverley Oakley, and Lexxie Couper - for this journey. Tracie and Mel, extra special thanks for taking a crazy idea and running with it.

- Joel, a brave man who took us on, and Momentum.
- Editor extraordinaire, Sarah, who polished waffly sentences and deleted (more) repetition.
- My friends, Marg, Joy and Helen.
- My sisters, their families and my extended family.
- My best mates, E and T, who dragged me from the computer begging for their walks.
- My husband, the writing-widow, who supports my insane dreams and smiles tolerantly when I'm sure he'd often rather groan.
- Australian Romance Readers Association for their continued support of Aussie romance writers.
- Patti Roberts, Paradox Book Cover Design and Formatting, created the most gorgeous cover for this book that inspired me to get it finished. And then assisted with all I needed to do!
- Diane Cassar, Ainslie Paton, Kim Petersen and Jennie Jones for reading the updated version of this story.

To every person who reads the words I write, THANK YOU <3 My dream of a writing career hasn't been an easy life change, but is rewarded by an indescribable feeling any time someone enjoys my creations. Thank you.

Cate xo

DEDICATION

Jim, Pete and Steph

PART 1

*E*squire: When we meet what would you like to do?

When we meet? My heart skips a beat before accelerating to warp speed. He wants to meet me? My hands sweat and my vision is fuzzy. It's hard to see the screen, much less find the keys to type back to him.

We don't phone or Skype or anything else. We chat. Words. That's us. I'm happy with words, with faceless anonymity.

Condamine: How did we get to meeting? I thought this was just online fun.

Esquire: Don't you want to meet? Aren't you curious to see if what we have on here exists irl?

In real life. Goose bumps slide down my arms. *Oh my God.* If what we have online exists in real life, I'll sizzle into a wisp of smoke, never to be heard from again. Since the first moment he spoke to me in this chat room ten months ago, our friendship's been a conflagration. I burn with need every time I chat with this man—if he is a man. What we have couldn't possibly exist like this in real life. And yet, curiosity niggles.

CONDAMINE: THIS COULD NEVER EXIST IRL.

ESQUIRE: WHY NOT?

CONDAMINE: I'M MUCH SHYER IRL. I WOULD NEVER TELL YOU THE THINGS I HAVE.

ESQUIRE: BUT I ALREADY KNOW. I ALREADY KNOW YOU. THINK HOW GOOD IT COULD BE.

I don't want to think how good it could be. When I do, my stomach churns and my head hurts, so I take the easy way out and redirect the conversation to the mundane. Work is common ground. We both work in labs. Talking with someone who understands the pressure, the skills, the techniques is the best debrief. We laugh about eccentric colleagues with their strict routines and odd habits. We talk about life.

The minutes turn to hours. It's late and we both have to sleep.

After our goodnights, I see the words ESQUIRE SIGNS OUT and the tension that usually snaps when he signs out doesn't. My nipples remain so tight they throb. Squirming in the computer chair in my draughty lounge room doesn't help the moisture pooling between my thighs. How does he do this to me? I step outside the old rented farmhouse into the hectares of silence and stare up at the star-laden sky.

He knows me better than anyone. We have shared so much—our deepest secrets, darkest fantasies, greatest fears and loftiest dreams. It's the same as having a real-life friend in that we open up to each other, but this connection is stronger because the anonymity and lack of physical contact allows complete openness. No judgements, no shock. Sharing everything freely.

What if it *was* as good in real life? What if whatever burned between us online was the same face to face? Would I be able to survive that intensity?

Could I survive not knowing?

Weekends we don't chat. It's been our pact since we first met to ensure that we stay grounded in reality— although that seems to be slipping. This weekend makes for two days of total frustration where my mind constantly churns in circles. *I should meet him. I shouldn't.* I'm distracted. There's a knot in my stomach so big I can hardly eat.

Through sleepless nights I ponder, finding each day a different answer. I'm not sure I have the courage to make this real. Or, more precisely, the courage to find out if it's imaginary.

I could talk to friends but I'm embarrassed about meeting someone online. They'll laugh and I'll lose confidence. Mum's on the farm with Dad in outback Queensland. She might understand the feelings but the internet part will confuse her. She'll tell me that if someone isn't standing in front of me, I can't know them.

But I know Esquire. At the beginning of the year he said hello in the chat room and asked if I was from Queensland and now living in New South Wales. His insight, from seeing my name, was uncanny.

～

Monday night. Thank goodness, I can finally talk to him.

Seeing him log in makes my palms sweat—what if he's changed his mind? Nauseated, I swallow hard before greeting him. Small talk is difficult but I manage. I'm not asking about meeting, I'll wait for him to bring up the topic. I don't want to push if he was only kidding with me. Finally he broaches the subject.

ESQUIRE: HEY, HAVE YOU THOUGHT ABOUT WHAT WE MIGHT DO IF WE MET IRL?

CONDAMINE: I'M HAVING TROUBLE NOT THINKING ABOUT IT.

ESQUIRE: ARE YOU SAYING THAT IN A GOOD WAY?

CONDAMINE: I'M NOT SURE. IT DEPENDS WHEN YOU ASK ME—IF I'M BEING BRAVE OR SCARED AT THAT MOMENT.

ESQUIRE: SCARED? TELL ME WHAT'S FRIGHTENING. IT'S JUST ME. YOU KNOW ME.

I do know him. That's part of my hesitation. And I don't know him—that's the other part. He's Esquire. I'm Condamine. Two fake names. Two fake people who enjoy being together. Well, I know I'm not fake, I'm a braver version of me behind this alias, but is he himself?

What can I tell him? Should I be completely honest? Or partly honest and touch lightly on my fears?

CONDAMINE: I'M WORRIED IT'LL BE A TOTAL FAILURE AND WE'LL LOSE THIS.

ESQUIRE: BUT WHAT DO WE HAVE IF IT GOES NOWHERE? BE BRAVE. WE'LL TALK IT ALL THROUGH HERE FIRST. NOTHING'LL GO WRONG.

He is so blasé. It must be his sexual experience. I know from the stories he's told that he's been with many women. Months ago I told him I've only had one lover and we broke up years ago, but he might not believe that from the way our online sex ignites. I doubt he's ever been with a woman as sexually incompetent as I am.

Maybe I'll just pretend I'm okay with meeting. Then we can stop talking about it and I can stop freaking out.

CONDAMINE: OKAY.

ESQUIRE: SO WHAT SHALL WE DO WHEN WE MEET?

CONDAMINE: I DON'T KNOW, SPEND TIME RELAXING, TALK, GO TO THE MOVIES, COFFEE? WHAT DO YOU WANT TO DO?

ESQUIRE: NICE :) BUT I MEANT SEX. WHICH FANTASIES SHALL WE PLAY OUT?

Shit. Here am I on the 'have a nice weekend' thought and he's already bonking me. I'm so not ready for this. I'm far too plain, not in his league, too naïve, too inexperienced to play out fantasies—his or mine. Yet when I imagine his hands touching me, or his lips, I get goose bumps as if he really is doing it. There's an ache of constant arousal between my legs.

ESQUIRE: SORRY, DID I SCARE YOU AGAIN?

CONDAMINE: YES. I'M TOTALLY HOPELESS. I'M THINKING COFFEE AND YOU'RE THINKING SEX. SEE, THIS WILL NEVER WORK.

ESQUIRE: IT WILL IF YOU START THINKING ABOUT SEX AND STOP WORRYING :) SOME DAYS YOU HAVE NO TROUBLE DOING THAT.

CONDAMINE: YES, THE DAYS WHEN THIS IS ALL MAKE-BELIEVE.

ESQUIRE: IT'S NEVER BEEN MAKE-BELIEVE.

Shudders ripple along my spine.

It never has been make-believe for me either. There's something strong between us, a real connection. Can he feel that too, feel something for me? Him—with all his sexual exploits? Surely he sees this is not going anywhere. He couldn't feel like I do.

Esquire: There's no need to be worried. It's like every other game we've played. You'll love it and kick yourself for being scared.

Condamine: I guess so. That seems to be what happens.

Esquire: So, if you could pick one fantasy to act out for real, one we've talked about before or a new one, what would it be?

Condamine: To have sex. And you?

Esquire: Just plain old sex? Nothing else?

Condamine: Sex on the beach.

I hope sex on the beach sounds exciting enough. Plain sex is too ordinary, although it would be enough for me after years of no real-person sex. The beach is all I can think of at this moment. I'm not sure sex in public is something I really want to try but it sounds kind of exciting. *Doesn't it?*

We've talked of fantasies before, like sex with two men, or with a man and another woman, or watching two men fuck, but none I'd do for real. None I want to act out. They're fantasies for a reason—they're supposed to stay stuck in my head!

Esquire: Don't you live in Wagga Wagga?

Condamine: Yes, why?

Esquire: I was hoping you'd like to try this fantasy when we meet.

Condamine: We have a beach.

Esquire: Wagga has a beach? I thought it was inland?

Condamine: It is inland. We have a river and it has a beach. There's even a five o'clock wave.

Esquire: Now I know you're joking.

Condamine: Not about the beach :) How about you, what's your fantasy?

Esquire: I'm sure you can guess my fantasy.

Condamine: I'm sure I can't. Remember I'm the girl who thinks of having coffee :)

Esquire: It's pretty far from coffee. Sure you want to hear it?

Condamine: Go on. It's no doubt something we've done on here already.

Esquire: I'd like to have anal sex with an anal virgin.

Holy hell! My arms drop and hang lifelessly beside me. I don't think I can lift them back to the keyboard. Anal sex. Although it's intrigued me since I first thought about it ... or was introduced to thinking about it ... I'm not sure I'm game to try. It wasn't Esquire who planted the thought, it was a gay chef I worked with years ago. My first job after leaving home, where I finally found out the world was not as innocent as my country upbringing had led me to believe.

Esquire has spoken of his penchant for anal before, and he knows I've never tried it. His view is that anal is good birth control, and the tight sensation and its taboo nature are also mind-blowing. We've had anal sex online but that's very different to real life. Until recently, our cyber-sex was cerebral-sex. His words stimulated my imagination which stimulated my body. No penetration. No touching, on my part. Not like real sex at all.

Anal sex seems raw and intimate. I'm terrified even thinking about it. Yet that tingling, throbbing sensation through my body persists.

ESQUIRE: ARE YOU GAME? ;)

I have to pretend to be blasé like him, however I might really feel.

CONDAMINE: WILL IT BE AS GOOD AS ONLINE?

ESQUIRE: BETTER. MUCH BETTER. YOU'LL LOVE IT. HOW ABOUT IN TWO WEEKS? I HAVE A FEW DAYS OFF AND COULD COME AND VISIT YOU THEN.

A fortnight? A real time? Help! my brain screams, but my body isn't listening. Hard throbbing stones have replaced my nipples. A sudden pulse in my clit and subsequent gush of fluid lets me know what my body wants. Shame my brain isn't listening.

CONDAMINE: WHAT? I THOUGHT THIS WAS THEORETICAL ... NOW IT'S HAPPENING?

ESQUIRE: I'LL BOOK A MOTEL ROOM. NO PRESSURE. WE CAN MEET UP AND SEE WHAT HAPPENS. IT'LL ONLY HAPPEN IF YOU WANT IT TO.

And that is supposed to relieve me? This man makes me believe anything is possible. He makes me quiver reading the words he types on a screen, for heaven's sake. What will he be like in person? But I'm being cool. *Remember.*

Condamine: Okay.

Esquire: Excellent. I'll confirm details next week. Let's talk more about your fantasy.

Condamine: My fantasy's pretty easy. We've both had sex ... just not together and not at the Wagga beach. So it shouldn't be too difficult.

That sounds self-possessed and collected, doesn't it? I'm getting the hang of it, aren't I?

Esquire: It's your fantasy. We'll make it special.

Condamine: Thanks :) It'll be us having sex for real. Skin touching skin. My body against yours. Actions not words.

Holy fuck! Thinking about it is bad but typing it makes my clit pulse painfully. Squirming is not helping. I need the one-handed typing trick I'm beginning to master. I strip off, clothes pooling at my feet. A freshly-cut-grass scented breeze drifts through the open door and makes my skin tingle. No housemates, no close neighbours. The isolation makes me brave.

Esquire: Oh, there'll be words. I want you telling me what you want, how you feel, what's working, what needs to be different. No silent sex with me. When I'm licking your cunt I want to know you're enjoying it.

Imagine if he did that? I couldn't be quiet. I groaned when I read the words, and he's nowhere near to touching me, much less licking.

Condamine: Oh ... yes ... don't stop ...

I can't finish the sentence because my hands have

other things to do. I know he'll understand and keep talking dirty to me.

My fingers slip into the folds of my cunt and are immediately soaked. *Oh ... yes.* Labia opened wide, I skim the pad of my forefinger across my clit. *Yes!* The pulsing is rapid. Circling, increasing the pressure ... a tap against the tip and it's throbbing. I need him, his words, anything.

ESQUIRE: I'M GOING TO TAKE MY TIME, KEEP YOU ON EDGE UNTIL YOU'RE BEGGING TO COME. FIRST WITH MY HAND, THEN MY MOUTH AND IF YOU'RE GOOD, I'LL FUCK YOU WITH MY COCK. DEEP AND HARD.

CONDAMINE: PLZ

ESQUIRE: ARE YOU TOUCHING YOURSELF NOW?

CONDAMINE: YES

And it's not easy to type but I want to encourage him to keep typing to me.

ESQUIRE: YOU KNOW THAT MAKES ME SO HARD. IT'S SO HOT.

God, I'm so close I'm going to explode. My hand is soaking, clit pounding. Rubbing my clit isn't enough. I push two fingers inside, stretching my cunt as I push them in and out. The slurping-suck that once embarrassed me makes it even hotter. Esquire once told me he loves the sound of wet cunt being fucked. I think of that and I'm almost there.

ESQUIRE: IT'LL BE SO MUCH BETTER WHEN IT'S MY HAND RUBBING YOUR CLIT. MY FINGERS FUCKING YOU, STRETCHING YOU WIDE. MY COCK POUNDING INTO YOUR SOAKING SLICKNESS. AND I KNOW YOU'LL BE SOAKING. I BET YOU'RE WET NOW. I WISH I COULD

HEAR HOW WET YOU ARE AS YOU WORK YOUR FINGERS INSIDE YOU.

Oh hell. Wet—it's flowing from me. Fingers moving fast, thumb circling my clit. Stretched out in my chair, I'm so damn close.

ESQUIRE: I'LL BE THE ONE MAKING YOU WAIT. MAKING THE BIGGEST ORGASM OF YOUR LIFE SWIRL INSIDE YOU, BUILDING HIGHER AND HIGHER ...

Oh, please let me come.

ESQUIRE: UNTIL YOU'RE SCREAMING, BEGGING ME FOR YOUR RELEASE. BEGGING ME TO LET YOU COME ... YOU'RE GOING TO COME SO HARD, OVER AND OVER. I'M GOING TO LOVE WATCHING YOU COME HARD FOR ME.

Fuck yes! Two quick thrusts and my cunt convulses around my fingers while my clit explodes. Shards of pleasure spear through me, muscles convulsing in the pleasure dance. I'm left panting to catch my breath. Sated.

ESQUIRE: I'D LOVE TO BE THERE NOW, WATCHING YOU TOUCH YOURSELF. KNOWING I MADE YOU COME :)

It's taken some time for me to stop feeling ridiculous masturbating in front of the computer while reading his words. There's something wicked about him knowing what I'm doing that pushes me to a greater release. I couldn't touch myself at first, but over the past month I've lost that inhibition.

He gives me exactly what I need. I don't even want to think about how he knows. It's totally insane but my tension eases when we do this, whether I come or he does. Nipples that have been pinched tight for days relax. My clit stops screaming, my shoulders loosen.

Quickly, I clean my hand with the wet wipes I keep on the shelf above, before going back to typing.

CONDAMINE: THANKS. BUT I'LL NEVER BEG :)

ESQUIRE: HOW WAS THAT? :)

CONDAMINE: AWESOME, THANKS.

ESQUIRE: YOU'RE OKAY WITH THE REST?

CONDAMINE: MORE THAN OKAY.

And my body can't wait. My mind ... well ... it has other ideas, still.

ESQUIRE: YOU'RE SO HOT. YOU'RE GOING TO GO OFF LIKE NEW YEAR'S WHEN I'M DOING THIS FOR REAL WITH YOU. TOMORROW WE CAN TALK ABOUT THE REST. SLEEP WELL.

ESQUIRE SIGN OUT.

A shower and half a cup of peppermint tea later, my mind overrules my body. Bloody hell! I have a sex maniac coming to meet me when I know next to nothing about having sex with a person. What's worse, I'm going to have sex on the beach. I'm not an exhibitionist. I only thought of it because of the name of the cocktail.

I press the heel of my hand into my forehead. *What have I done?* Have I agreed to sex without ever seeing the guy? Not even knowing his real name? All the doubts that disappeared while I talked to him surface again. *Oh my God.* Have I also really committed to anal sex? *Fuck!*

Even with all these fears, my body's tingling as if it wants all this to happen. Thinking about sex with Esquire has desire pounding through me but my mind is screeching no. There is complete discord between the two. I haven't met him yet, have never even heard his voice. All I've done is read his words, his thoughts. If they are his thoughts. If he is a 'he'. If he really exists. *Damn my mind.*

I can't possibly be horny again. I can usually go for weeks without orgasm. I get up from the chair and stalk about the house and garden trying to alleviate the tension of my pounding clit. It only makes things worse. My skin sweats and prickles. Pulse rate closing in on rapid. I'm going to expire before I get to meet him. I fan my fingers through the air near my face to try to cool myself down.

I add batteries to my shopping list and take my vibrator to bed. It's not him, but it's more like him than my hand.

Our online meetings are not only about sex. It's a normal relationship, except for not seeing each other. We discuss work, religion, politics, literature, films, and the minutiae of life: bills, his flatmate, food. When we're talking it's fast, like there is so much to say and so little time. It thrills me to be so open with someone, to know a person intimately so that I understand their mind, their way of thinking. I've never felt this close to anyone before. I make friends easily but never like this.

The fortnight crawls by. We keep to our schedule and our chats are no different to before, except there is an extra excitement bubbling through me. The bubbles swell, filling me with that heady feeling you get drinking sparkling wine through a straw.

And then it's our last chat on the day before our meeting. My mind is still struggling but my body is mostly in control.

ESQUIRE: HELLO :) I CAN'T STAY FOR LONG BUT I WANTED TO MAKE SURE WE'RE STILL OKAY FOR TOMORROW.

CONDAMINE: YOU'RE STILL COMING?

ESQUIRE: OF COURSE. I WOULDN'T MISS THIS FOR THE WORLD. ARE YOU READY FOR ME?

CONDAMINE: YES AND NO. BUT I'LL BE THERE.

ESQUIRE: I KNOW YOU WILL :)

Nervously, I click my nail against the edge of the keyboard. I have never been tongue-tied before. Do you still call it tongue-tied when you're typing? I exhale, jutting my bottom lip so air expels across my face. I need to be calm. I'm meeting him tomorrow and I have no idea what to say. My stomach is twisted tighter than my nipples or clit and I can't decide if it's nerves or anticipation. My mind is panic-stricken but it knows it has been outvoted. I can only hope it doesn't decide to rule once he's here.

CONDAMINE: YOU KNOW HOW TO GET HERE? HOW TO GET TO THE CAFÉ, SCRIBBLES?

ESQUIRE: OF COURSE. MY ROUTE'S ALL PLANNED. HAS BEEN SINCE YOU TOLD ME WHERE YOU LIVED.

CONDAMINE: YOU MEAN YOU'VE ALWAYS MEANT TO VISIT ME?

ESQUIRE: YES. AND YOU'VE ALWAYS WANTED ME TO COME.

It's a statement but I answer him anyway.

CONDAMINE: YES.

I'm excited, elated, petrified and full of anticipation. All at once. All jumbled up so I can't think. I can't eat either. Thinking of all the mind-blowing online sex we've shared, I can't wait for him to get here. But what if there's nothing between us when we meet? No chemistry?

CONDAMINE: ARE YOU SURE WE'LL FIND EACH OTHER? WE DON'T NEED TO WEAR CERTAIN CLOTHES OR EXCHANGE PHOTOS?

ESQUIRE: WE KNOW EACH OTHER SO WELL I'M SURE I'LL RECOGNISE YOU. THIS TIME TOMORROW WE'LL MEET. I CAN'T WAIT.

It seems crazy that you would be able to identify someone from typing to them, but I give him the benefit of the doubt. Scribbles isn't huge, so chances are he will find me even if he has to speak to all the women in the café.

CONDAMINE: SEE YOU TOMORROW. SAFE TRAVELS.

Now the wait begins in earnest. I just have to listen to my body, quieten my mind and turn up. We are meeting in public first, with a friend nearby. I'm not allowing him into my house if he's a nutter, and I half expect him to be. My friend's a cook at Scribbles and he'll do brotherly protection if I need it. I need only order a double serve of salad and he'll muscle me away from a maniac.

Seated in Scribbles at a table towards the back, I watch the front door. I'm an hour early because I couldn't stay at work a moment longer. You need to be precise in a laboratory and today I was all thumbs. Slides slipped from my hands while I tried to stain them. Microscopes wouldn't focus. Cells misbehaved. It was torture. Even my co-workers asked if I was coming down with something. I left early to avoid any major disasters. I cannot let my work suffer because I'm intoxicated by nervous lust.

The clock in the café is slower than the clocks at home and the lab. The hands hardly move. My pot of tea arrives but my stomach is twisted into knots so tight that even tea isn't travelling through. My first sip gets stuck about mid-chest.

I pick up *The Daily Advertiser* and try to read the cover story but it isn't anything that grabs me. I usually read the paper cover to cover. It's the best way to know a place. Today it's not capturing my attention. I turn the page. Nothing interesting. I survey the coffee shop; no one new since I last looked. I turn the page. Still nothing to read. The door clicks open. A woman and her child. I turn the page.

Why is it when you wait for something, time slows to a standstill? Does Father Time check what you're doing and juggle the clocks accordingly? He's a perverse bastard.

After forty impossibly slow minutes the door clicks open. I look up from the dull newspaper and stare without breathing, my heart on pause. He's around my age, tall, brown hair, brown eyes, tanned skin, strong face with a determined look. It has to be him.

Gulping a breath that kickstarts my pulse, I watch him scan the room. Dark eyes stop at me. Go on but come straight back. He stops and stares. Our eyes meet. *Esquire.* The beginning of a smile breaks across his full lips. My mouth mirrors his smile.

Esquire strides towards me. Loping on legs so long I have to strain my neck to keep my gaze on his as he gets closer. His shoulders are wide, impossibly wide. His face angular, shadowed but welcoming. It's his eyes that capture me; they're mesmerising. Not the colour but the intensity. He looks at me as if there is no one else in the world. I could lose myself in those dark depths.

I stand as he reaches the table, my hand extends towards him. This isn't part of the plan. Something's possessed me. I want to touch him. Make sure he is real.

"Esquire." Smiling as I say his name, my hand brushes his and any other words I may have spoken are caught somewhere deep in my body. Probably with that sip of tea, still twisted in the knots in my chest.

"Condamine. Hello." Two distinct words. The first light as air, as if he exhaled a thought. The second stronger, deeper, smiling with welcome.

He leans towards me. Inhaling, I bring his scent inside me—citrus and musky male. *He really is here.* While I'm still processing, pillow-soft lips meet mine. Lightly. The barest hint of stubble grazes my skin. The dark taste of coffee lingers on his lips. There is no pressure to the kiss. It's a welcome, a greeting, and as soft as silk brushing against me. I want to draw him closer and feel that silken touch across my whole body. But I'm in a cafe. We've just met.

He sits opposite me, my fingertips still held lightly in his, a table between us. The hold is light, intense but comfortable. We don't speak. I don't feel the need. His gaze catches mine and won't let go. Honesty shines from his face. He is not as comfortable about meeting me as the typed conversations led me to believe. Nerves lurk inside him. But the smile that lingers on his lips and lights his eyes tells me he is pleased to be here. Pleased to be with me, to see me, to hear me, to touch me. I bask in his gaze. I don't mind if he reads every bit of terror I've felt the last few weeks. I don't mind if he knows how much anticipation has built inside me. I don't care if he sees how affected by him I am. He knows me better than anyone ever has.

A head appears from the kitchen, an eyebrow raised in question. I smile and give a brief shake of my head. I don't need brotherly protection.

"Did you want to finish your tea, or should we go?" Esquire asks.

He must read minds. I was wondering how to suggest we leave. It's not surprising. He could read my mind across half the continent, through cyberspace. I suppose it's easier now with scant inches between us.

I nod and collect my purse. Still holding my tingling hand, he leads me out of the café and onto the street. He doesn't seem in any hurry to let me go and I like being held. It's comforting and secure, which is crazy because I've just met him.

I shake my head, trying to find the sense I once had, but it's gone. My body is blazing with lust. A tiny part of my brain screams *this is crazy*. I tug my fingertips from his hand. "Does this feel normal?" My voice isn't as shaky as I expected.

His hand rests lightly on my shoulder and the connection is now the centre of my universe. His voice is smooth, like aged red wine. "It feels perfectly normal. Like we've met a thousand times already. That is weird, isn't it?"

"Everything about us is weird." Who meets a man after talking to them for almost a year on the internet? Who meets a man after learning all his thoughts, dreams and fantasies? Oh, Lord, don't think of that. *Fantasies.*

We gaze at each other for too long before Esquire breaks the silence. "I'm still not sure I believe there's a Wagga beach. Will you show me?" His question is innocently asked so if anyone heard they would think nothing of it but there's nothing innocent in my interpretation.

"I haven't decided if I'm taking you."

"Yes, you have." His dark gaze challenges. Not in a way that makes me want to hide but in a way that tells me he knows how I think. It sends delicious shudders through me. *He knows me so well.* I find myself dropping my gaze. He's right. The moment I saw him I knew he was coming not only to the beach but to my home.

"Do you want to follow, or come with me?" As soon as the words leave my mouth my stomach does the old Eskimo roll. *How could I have said that?* A suggestive leer appears in his eye and the corner of his lip quirks. He says nothing but I know his answer. We travel together.

My car is close so I beep it open with the remote key. He laughs before turning towards me. "You drive a bright yellow beetle?"

"It's my childhood dream to own a 'Herbie' car. No

laughing or you can't travel with me." His laughter changes to a grin and he slips into the passenger seat of my Volkswagen.

"We could walk," I tell him while I drive, "but it'll be dark soon and I don't like walking around town at night."

It only takes a few minutes to drive to the beach. We turn left and wind our way down the hill to the car park. It is dusk. In front of us the deserted park, playground and amenities are lit by a single light. The night air is cooling. I turn the ignition off and reach to undo my seatbelt when Esquire's fingers touch my hand, making me jump.

"This is the beach?" He's disappointed. He doesn't believe me. I knew he would be like that, too. This area is deceiving. I smile to myself. *At least I know him as well as he knows me.*

"The river's to the left of the park, protected by the large river gums." I grin, reach across and ... touch my fingertip to the tip of his nose. "Trust me."

Bloody hell! I flick off my seatbelt and bounce from the car. That was a bit too intimate. His lips pouted just before I touched his nose. I very nearly touched my fingers against his lips. I nearly kissed him. Online I would have kissed him. In person there's a reserve that holds me back but it nearly didn't kick in. I nearly did online things. Should there be a difference? I don't know.

I've got to calm myself.

Striding towards the beach, I consciously slow my breathing. I know he'll follow.

At the edge of the grass, I'm toeing my boots off when I hear his exclamation behind me.

"Holy shit. I thought you were kidding."

I laugh and tension flows from me. There's the hint of relief in his voice as if the beach was a test of my honesty and I've passed.

I peel my socks off, leaving them tucked in my boots on the edge of the grass, before rolling up my jeans. I step onto the beckoning white sand and spin once, arms wide.

"Welcome to the Wagga beach!"

At the river's edge, I stare into the murky depths, looking for calm. The swirling water catches the last rays of sunlight. Deep shadows are cast across the river from the surrounding trees. Further out, where it's deeper, the water races, causing eddies to circle and spin. That's how I'm feeling—churned up.

My body tingles as the air moves behind me. His body is shading me. Although I feel his heat, when I lean back I can't touch him. He is close but not close enough to crowd me. Surrounded by his warmth, I close my eyes and soak in pleasure. My body is once again in control.

The river always relaxes me and his presence adds to the soothing atmosphere. My hands dangle by my sides. His fingers brush mine before his arms encircle me. I lean back and now I find his chest and shoulders. I have only just met him, yet I feel like I've found the place I want to be.

My body's relaxed, but my brain is having a minor meltdown. *We shouldn't fit so easily together. It shouldn't be this comfortable.* Fortunately, these thoughts shut down when his luscious lips touch my neck and nibble lightly on my ear lobe. His breath dances across my ear before he says, "Jeans aren't the best thing to wear to have sex on the beach. A great big skirt is so much easier."

I should have thought to be sexy but I stayed in my work clothes because it was easier than deciding what to wear. I should have some witty comeback. Instead I laugh. Snorting loudly enough to scare the birds from their roosts. *Idiot!*

"I did warn you I had no idea."

"And I told you not to worry."

I drop my gaze, staring at the sand and his bare feet. *How can I be eager for sex when I'm so inexperienced?* My gaze runs over his long feet and toes. Such defined bone structure. They're sexy as sin with the dark smattering of hair across the bottom of each toe and a thin line edging along the arch of each foot towards the ankle. Biting my lip, I slowly look up, twisting around to meet his eyes. Something sizzles within them, setting my body afire.

"Do you have sex with strangers often?" I was only thinking the words but suddenly they're fired at him, surprising him almost as much as me. I hate feeling out of my depth, and I am so far out it's like I'm caught in one of the deep eddies in the river.

"You're no stranger to me." He reaches out and strokes his thumb across my cheekbone towards my nose, then follows it to the edge of my lip before curling his fingers beneath my chin and tilting my face to his. Muscles liquefy at his caress. "I've always known you. From the moment we talked online. Meeting you in person has only made that stronger." His gaze bores into mine, so strongly. I have to believe his words, although it is difficult. Everything you hear tells you that you can't meet people online and trust them. But I do trust him.

"If you're not ready, it's no trouble. We have four days to get to know each other. I just didn't want to waste time if we both wanted the same thing." His hand drops to squeeze my shoulder.

If I'm honest, I want him. I don't care to sit and make small talk. But that is not what you do. I'd feel loose, immoral, a floozy. Oh, dear God in heaven. I sound like my grandmother.

I gather every shred of courage in me.

"I have a towel in the car, would that do as a skirt? Should I go get it?"

For long seconds only our gazes touch and then we're together. Our bodies meet as if it's not the first time. We fit together like jigsaw pieces. His lips close over mine. My hips nestle into his. My breasts, against his chest, press into the embrace. It is exquisite. And the kiss is scorching. Our tongues duel slowly, twisting and sliding against each other until his taste fills my brain. I can't stop kissing him. I snatch breaths as our lips move. Drag air through my nose when I can. Breathing is irrelevant. Kissing is all that matters.

But before long, kissing is not enough. Writhing against his body, my hands slip beneath his T-shirt to tour his back, from buttocks to nape. Every muscle against his spine is honed hard. My fingertips delight in each bump and hard ridge before my hands splay across his shoulder blades. When that is no longer enough, my nails skim against the edges of his muscles. And all the time the kissing continues, becomes hotter, until it snatches not only my breath but my sanity.

His hands slide beneath my shirt and up across my breasts. Arching my back lets me press into his hands and not lose his lips. His fingers tweak my nipples through the lace of my bra until they are so tightly clenched they're throbbing. The long deep moan is mine. Before I can apologise there's a snap, and freedom. My breasts spill loose. My bra is undone and his hands lift, weigh and knead my heavy breasts. Nothing compares. Online sex gave me all the words but his touch makes words insignificant.

I want him. Now. This stranger who knows my mind, my body. I pull away. Inching back a step at a time, dragging my lips free, my body away from his.

"Can we move behind those rocks?" My breath comes in gasps. It doesn't sound sexy at all. It sounds like sheer desperation.

"No, let's have sex here, on the beach." His voice is a whisper-like caress and it takes a while for the words to push through the lust-haze.

I can't have sex in public. I take a step away. Quickly, I glance around, making sure there's no one here. We're alone. Sanity flows through me. It must have come on the cool night air or danced in on moonbeams, because it wasn't there a moment ago.

He comes behind me and touches his fingertips against the small of my back. There is no pressure. "I don't want to hide. I want to see you in the moonlight. I want to hear the water gurgling past. I want to fuck you on the soft sand. There's no one here. Let's live out your fantasy." Each sentence has me drawn into his web further and further.

The rich red-wine smoothness of his voice is intoxicating. His words call to my body, arousing each cell as if they've been trained. I turn around so my lips touch his again, lightly at first, but then the kiss ignites. I want to live out my fantasy too.

It's a tangle of fingers and hands as we shed each other of clothes, as if we have done it before. We work together well. And then we're naked. Moonbeams spotlight the pale flesh of his torso, showing me his outdoors sports tan with shirt, shorts and sock marks. Musculature I had felt earlier is delineated in the soft light, looking even more honed. The sweep of his chest is dusted with dark hair, a line travels across his stomach and a short bush surrounds his erection. His cock juts proudly at me, his balls hanging tight between strong thighs spread shoulder-width apart. I chuckle. "You're posing for me."

"And what do you think?" His teeth gleam and I'm sure his eyes would be sparkling if they were not in shadow.

"Better than I ever imagined." I take a step closer to him, happy to keep looking but a little self-conscious that he is also looking at me.

"Better than you told me."

I lift an eyebrow. What's better than I told him? Before I can ask, he tells me. "You sold yourself short. You're gorgeous."

I'm not sure I believe him—no one has ever called me gorgeous—but the confidence his words give me sets my heart soaring. I stretch along his body, my nipples grazing across his chest. Wrapping my arms around his neck, I whisper my thanks against his mouth. And then we're writhing, kissing, tasting, licking, sucking, touching. It is crazy, frenzied, and I love every second of the wildness.

Soon that's not enough, and we're on our knees in the sand, then lying side by side, captured by each other's gaze, touching almost reverently. The rough caress of the sand is a direct contrast to his gentle touch. The cool sand beneath me opposes the heat of his body against mine. It's sensory overload. It's ... *ohhhh* ...

His mouth settles between my legs and he laps against my labia. Huge shudders rip through me. *A million times better than online.* My legs part further, giving him an invitation he doesn't need. I press my hips upwards as his mouth homes in. *Fuck!* His mouth is hot and wet but my body is cooled by the sand and air. He licks along the heated length of my cunt and I can no longer feel my body. Closing his lips on my clit, he hums lightly and I soar. So high I don't know where the rest of me has gone. I'm my clit. There is nothing else of me.

He lets go of my tender flesh and I gulp a breath of cool air. My body temperature decreases, back to a level I can handle. But the respite is short-lived. His tongue fucks me. Pressing into me, then withdrawing. I squirm, pushing my hips up, following his tongue as it withdraws. I want him inside me. His tongue fucks me hard. I'm writhing and moaning. Coarse sand grates against my shoulder blades as I dig down to lift my hips further. It's stinging but I don't care. I don't want him to ever stop kissing me ... down there.

But he does.

He moves up my body, kissing every centimetre he passes. His tongue drags across skin. His teeth nip at fleshy parts. Until he kisses, nips or licks it, that body part does not seem to exist. He brings it to life. My body is no longer mine but there for his pleasure—and although my brain skids on that thought, my body overrides it.

Once his lips find mine, it's exquisite. I taste myself mixed with his coffee flavour and male scent. A musky overtone I devour.

His body settles over me. Hips brushing against mine cause me to arch for closer contact. His chest rubs against my breasts. Chest hair scrapes across nipples so sensitive it's as if they are raw. His legs tangle with mine. His swollen cock presses against my stomach. Strong, thick, hard.

I part my legs, wrapping them around his hips to urge him inside me. I want to feel him fill me, fuck me. But his fingers are there, teasing. He presses his fingers into my body. It is no invasion. I want him a part of me. His fingers stretch me, excite me. I arch upwards, straining for more. I need to feel full. I need his cock inside me. At the moment it is brushing against my inner thigh, tormenting me.

"Please, fuck me." I beg. Something I told him I'd never do but tonight it comes naturally. Rolls from my lips before his tongue plunders my mouth.

Finally, fumbling in his jeans lying beside us, he grabs a condom and within seconds is protected. His cock presses against my vagina. My heart pounds, my body tenses, my clit flutters hopelessly. I push towards him, eager to feel him inside, tightening my legs around his hips to pull him closer, deeper. His hand soothes along the length of my buttock and thigh. "Easy. Easy." His words soothe me none. Burning with lust, I want him to take me, claim me, fuck me. Now. Hard. Fast. Furious.

But he won't. As much as I beg he refuses. Teasing me until the sand abrades my back and I have to stop writhing. Frustrated tears well. It is sensory overload and I can't handle it. A finger brushes across my cheekbone and I blink before focusing on his gaze. His lips form a small smile and his cock slips inside. No thrust, just the head pushed in. Relief surges like rain after the long buildup to a storm. I expect him to thrust but he withdraws too soon. Much too soon. Before I can growl my displeasure he swipes the slickened head against my clit, back and forth, until my moans are incoherent begging pleas.

When I can take no more teasing he thrusts inside me. I arch off the sand. Bliss. Pure bliss. Filled. There's a long moment of silent stillness as we adjust to our coupling. Gazes lock as tightly as our bodies.

Yap, yap, yap, yap!

We both freeze. Tense. Our eyes wide and locked together.

Awareness hits. Grit grinds beneath me. The night air whispers across my skin, making sure I remember I'm naked. Naked in a public place. The moonlight makes us beacons. We're going to be caught having sex on the beach. These aren't butterflies in my stomach, they're vultures circling.

Esquire moves to cover me completely. He lowers his

chest over mine, his face over mine. He wads our clothes together and packs them like a wall beside me. If anyone comes they might only see him.

Little puffy dog breaths arrive just before a wet nose presses to the side of my face. *Oh god.* A dog is usually on the end of a leash. Scrunching my eyes tight, I chant in my head, 'Please don't let us get caught,' over and over. My heart is beating so loudly the whole of Wagga must be able to hear.

Esquire shoos the dog away with a whispered hiss and a flick of his hand. A distant voice calls. The little dog trots away. The vultures crash to the pit of my stomach and drown in waves of relief. That was close, too close. My brain goes into panic mode, overruling anything my body was feeling.

"Oh my God, I thought we were caught," I whisper.

I try to wriggle from beneath Esquire's body, but he nips my ear lobe. "Quit moving or this isn't going to last long." His voice is a tense growl. I quit moving. His cock is still inside me and the fear has aroused him further. His cock is like steel. *Oh dear God.* I was about to give up, but he is primed and ready to go.

I look into his eyes, catch his lower lip between mine and slide my tongue across the plump flesh before releasing it. "Who wants it to last?" My scratchy, seductive voice surprises me. I sound like a siren. His response makes me feel like one too. He growls against my ear, catches my legs in his arms, kneels up and thrusts into me, holding me tightly against his pounding hips. The angle gives a deep, satisfying penetration. In seconds, I forget the dog. I forget the sand beneath me. I forget everything except the power of him.

His thrusting is hard, fast and furious. Perfect. Just what I need. Each stroke pushes his cock deeper inside, stretching me, completing me. The wet sucking sounds of sex drown the gurgling river. A deep thrust and his cock bangs against my cervix. I half-moan, half-scream, arching beneath him as my muscles clench, capturing his cock as he thrusts deep inside me.

His breath catches, a tiny moan breaks his lips, his hips jerk in fast spasms before they shoot forward and the bones of his hips press deeper into the backs of my thighs. The shuddering release of his cock triggers my muscles to spasm.

"Oh, yes—" My unfinished cry is caught by my orgasm. A tsunami of pleasure bears down on me. My hips rock, muscles clenching and releasing. White noise, like static, scratches at my mind. Colours, like a perfect outback sunset, burst behind my eyes. Every muscle in my body screams tight, holds, holds, then releases.

I'm loose. Limp. Languid.

We are both panting, trying to collect our breath and cool our bodies.

My usual orgasms aren't like that.

He eases me flat against the sand. His hands slide down my legs as he lowers me. He pulls his cock from inside me and the loss is softened when he follows my body to the sand, resting over me with exquisite care and tenderness. A single tear leaks from the corner of my eye and scurries down the side of my face to the sand. Esquire is all I hoped he might be.

"Sorry." He presses his lips softly over each eyelid, my nose then lips. "I'm so sorry. I wanted that to be much slower." His voice is a whisper.

I smile at him. The dark shadows make his face unreadable. "I might have died if you made it any slower." His teeth break through the shadow, gleaming. I see a smile emoticon in my mind. He always smiles after we have sex online. It is all so similar but so different. Better. A gazillion times better.

"We could go slowly next time." I keep my tone light. I don't want to be pushy. I've had the most amazing sex of my sheltered life. I don't want to appear greedy for more —although I am.

"You can guarantee that." His teeth still gleam as he leans forward and presses a soft kiss to my mouth. I didn't think I could feel any happier but this ... it means he wants more too. We're going to have more sex. *Oh my God.* I'm going to ...

"How about a quick swim before you take me home?" His words interrupt my thought. As I focus, he rummages in his jeans and pulls out a small plastic bag, removes the condom and disposes of it in the bag.

"Are you always well prepared? Condom and rubbish bag?"

His lips twitch into a ready grin. "I was hoping I'd get lucky on the beach." He shrugs. "I didn't want to leave it lying around. I couldn't think of anything else."

My heart does a little flip-flop. He planned this for me. He even thought about protection and rubbish disposal.

A flick of his finger against my nose grabs my

attention. "How about that swim? I'm all sweaty and sandy." He looks magnificent glistening in the moonlight.

"You're sandy? I'm covered in it. I'm sure I've loofahed two layers of skin off." I peel myself from the emery-board beach and stretch my legs to get them moving again. There are slight muscle twinges but I am far too exalted to worry about them. He turns me around and manoeuvres me so he can see my back in the moonlight. Splashing water to wash off the majority of the sand, he inspects me.

"No permanent damage. But your skin gleams with good health." He swats my bottom before smacking a kiss to my bare neck. I must have known him forever. There is no way I could feel this relaxed with someone I have only just met. Laughing, I follow him into the river.

We swim in the shallows until we are freezing. Then we rub ourselves dry with jeans and we dress. He slides his hand around mine so naturally as we walk back to the car. It is incredible how well things have gone. I cannot believe I'm this happy—sated but still aroused.

"One fantasy down, one to go." My voice makes it sound like I'm gloating but I'm not. I can't get the thought out of my head that we will be having sex again, soon.

He stops me. A momentary flutter of concern fills me but his face is not that of a man leaving. He is as hungry as I am. "You think we only have one to go?" His voice is serious, not joking like mine. A tiny frisson sparks through me. Not quite fear, not quite lust, more awareness.

"Are we doing more fantasies? I only remember talking about two."

"Why limit ourselves? We can act out every fantasy we've ever had, and develop new ones. The world is ours." His grin is infectious. I follow suit. But smiling back at him causes laughter to bubble out of me. Loud laughter. It stops suddenly when my mind takes control. *I don't know his name.* My mental head-slap is hard. I'm fucking a man I still don't know. *How stupid am I? Still.*

"Will I ever find out your name?"

"Of course—I completely forgot. It feels like I know you already. I'm Sebastian Kurt Goodwin."

"Caitlyn Rose Bloss." We shake hands like a formal introduction and it's too funny. I start laughing again. I've just had sex before I know his name. I'm insane. And what's more, Esquire suits him. Sebastian seems too long and formal. Seb. He's a Seb. "Can I call you Seb?" I'm grinning like a loon.

"You can call me whatever you like, Caitlyn." He winks. "Caitlyn rolls off the tongue. Not like Condamine."

Happiness explodes inside. I have so much energy I need to release. I spin circles on the grass, round and around. Arms outstretched. "Woooohoooo!" I spin until Seb's arms catch hold and stop me. He's laughing and I feel no shame at my childishness. He captures my lips and we kiss until my head really spins.

No word does justice to the elation that fills me. I am like an over-filled balloon waiting to burst. We have four days to indulge our every fantasy.

"Did you really book a motel room?"

He chuckles and nods. "I wasn't one hundred per cent sure this would work."

I hit his shoulder with a flat hand. "You weren't? You sure sounded confident to me."

He grins and plants a kiss on my nose. "I guess you'd better drop me back to my car so I can check in."

I stare at him to be sure but I've already made the decision. "Would you rather cancel the booking and come home with me? I live in an old farmhouse at the edge of town. It's not flash but it's private."

He wraps his arms around me, sliding his hands down my back before cupping my butt. A shudder ripples through me. "Are you worried about the next fantasy?"

Looking into his concerned eyes, I answer honestly. "Yes." Half a heartbeat later I add, "But I'm not worried about being with you."

Seb is in my house. In my house. He walks past my computer, pauses and grins. One look at that grin and I flee. There's too much in that smile. Too much knowledge. Too much pleasure. Too much hope.

Heading through the lounge to the bedrooms, I stop and Seb's bag hits the back of my leg. I hadn't heard him follow so closely.

"Sorry," he murmurs and catches the duffel to his side.

"It's my fault." I'm being all kinds of brave, so I mutter, "I don't know where to put you." Me, sounding like a nincompoop, is something he became accustomed to as Esquire, so I hope he can handle it as Seb.

My hand waves between my bedroom and the spare room. I'm sure my face tells him more about my dilemma than words and actions.

"How about I put my bag in the spare room, and we work out the rest later?"

Breath whooshes. That's a plan. A good plan. He's a

visitor, he isn't moving in. He'll have space in there, privacy. My clit pulses, reminding me that I desperately want him in my bed. Or at least my body wants that, my mind is still arguing.

After he carelessly tosses his bag on the bed, he turns and looks at me. His eyes aren't just looking at the outside, he's staring deeply into me, as if trying to work out who I am in the deepest parts of myself. I don't know why he needs to study me for that. He knows me inside out and backwards.

"I could do with a shower," he states.

I jump. "Of course. That'll warm you up." His eyebrow lifts and heat warms my chest before flaming upwards. He doesn't need warming, he's as hot as hell.

I spin away, burying my head in the linen cupboard and digging out a towel and face cloth. An inordinate amount of time passes, not because I can't choose between colours, but because I have to get my flaming face under control. Have to calm my pulsing body. Have to settle my crazed mind.

I've no hope of the last two things.

Giving up my quest for sanity and control, I turn and pass him the towel. His gaze meets mine, again it's as if he sees into my soul.

"Care to wash my back?"

Wash his back?

My mind stutters, then stalls. They're the code words. The words we'd played with online. The ones which say that he's keen, he wants to act out his fantasy, and all I need do is accept, shower with him, and grant him his fantasy.

Anal sex.

I'm not ready for that.

"I'll put the kettle on," I say in a hurry, before turning and dashing three steps away. Then my stomach knots and my head twists.

He's got that grin again. The one he had when he spied my computer. The one that promises the world. As he reaches for the hem of his t-shirt, I walk so quickly out of there I may have run.

Heart pounding, legs like jelly, breath difficult to suck in and push out, I thrust the kettle under the tap and fill it. I flick the switch and as my arm brushes my chest, my nipples scrape against my bra and a shudder rips right through me. My lips part and a low moan attempts to diffuse my angst.

Moaning is no antidote to the frustration, the need.

Seb is naked in my shower and I'm fluffing with a kettle. He made my fantasy come true, and I'm stalling on his. Why?

I'm scared. Not of him. He's been gentle, considerate, sweet, kind, even if impossibly hot and incredibly sexy.

I'm terrified of me, of the unknown, of failing him, of not living up to a fantasy.

What an idiot.

I have the opportunity of a lifetime and I'm not taking it. Not gobbling up every second of this four-day adventure.

I strip off my shirt, dropping it on the way to the shower. My bra follows. Jeans are shed, along with pants. I walk through that open bathroom door. One deep breath. "Would you like me to wash your back?" I sound like me, sort of. A version of me who's lost their voice, or smoked ten packs a day, or screamed at the footy too long.

His head pokes around the screen. His eyes widen as he looks me up and down. "I'd love you to."

I step into his body, beneath the spray, and every part of me heats at once. And that's before he kisses me. Devours me.

Or maybe we devour each other.

The way his lips move, and his tongue explores, shows me how restrained he'd been with our earlier kisses. I consume his mouth as he does mine. I taste his tongue, closing my lips over it and sweetly sucking. Oh, the freaking head spin of that. While I'm spinning out, he takes over. When we pause for a breath, I flick my tongue across his lower lip before sucking it between mine. Ignition. Our lips meet, move, mash and meld, over and over. My tongue dances across his, slides, twists and twines with his. His taste is deliciously addictive and that's something I'd never imagined in all the online kissing.

Kissing him is a million times better in real life. I never want to stop.

He soaps me, while we kiss. His hands skim over the light slick foam coating me. A soft caress and I'm completely addicted.

"Fuck," he groans as I stretch his lip before popping it from between mine. "Your fucking mouth." It's a curse as much as a compliment. It makes my heart soar. I suspect I resemble a cat having eaten cream.

When we take a small step apart, I notice his cock. I mean, sure I noticed it before. It's been pressing against me the entire time, but I hadn't had a chance to stop and look. My breath's snatched from me.

His cock stands, proudly pulsing. Upright. Out from his flat stomach. Thick. Long. Begging for my touch. Tentatively, I reach for it, my fingers close slowly around.

"Christ." Although his exhale makes it seem like he's relaxed, there's not a thing that isn't tense. His body is rigid. The flesh enfolded in my fingers is turgid. His shoulders are pressed back, held tight, as if bracing for a blow. His jaw is clamped, a muscle pulses near his ear. "Don't fucking move." The words seem gritted from between his teeth.

I hold still. Unsure about what I've done wrong. Does he mean I have to keep my hand on his cock, or should I loosen and let it go?

He can hardly breathe. I need to let go. My grip loosens.

I bite my lips together. I've fucked this up. So quickly. All that planning and I've ruined it. I duck my head, afraid tears might fall. At least they might be mistaken for water droplets.

My hand slides down his length.

"Do that but grasp it hard again." He's kind of gasping for breath, like when we were at the beach after the dog disturbed us.

When I work that out, my fear abates. I grip his cock, hard, and stroke. It isn't easy to tug his flesh while holding tightly. *The soap.* I grab it and suds up his stomach, drawing bubbles beneath my hand onto his cock. My hand glides across his skin better, while keeping my grasp tight. *Winning!*

"Fuck, yes." His head's thrown back and his lips part. As he arches backwards, slightly, all the muscles of his stomach become tight and ripple. *Magnificent.*

In all the times I'd jerked him off online, it's never been this good. The look on his face, of bliss or rapture or something incredibly amazing, is making me wet. Not shower wet, aroused wet. As if by stroking his cock, I'm stroking myself.

His growl rumbles right through my body and vibrates against my clit. "Faster. Please. Fuck." His hand splats against the shower wall covering a whole bunch of tiles. His fingers aren't completely flat but slightly raised, like that hand is holding every bit of his weight. His eyes clench, his body jerks, and I squat before him. Awkwardly because I didn't want to change my grip or the movement.

I slide my tongue across the head of his cock as it thrusts through my grip. Then close my mouth over the head and suck.

"F-U-C-K." The word comes out timed to the pulsation of his cock. His body jerks hard. His cock slides from between my lips, but my hand still clenches and strokes. A few judders then cum shoots, oozing over my hand, slicking his cock. I keep moving, like I'm milking every drop from him.

On my knees, arm aching, I can't stop staring. At his face as he comes. At his cock as it spurts. At all the muscles rippling and tensing in between. It's a feast. I will never forget this moment.

Everything is impressive but watching the milky spurts ejaculate as his body spasms with each surge, is powerful. I've caused this. I pleasured him. I was in control. Nothing had prepared me for this moment. Not even all those hours of online sex.

The pulsating and swearing slows. His cock gives a half-hearted squirt and instinctively I ease my grip. I keep some pressure and slow movement, right up until his hand closes on my wrist. A little pressure and I glance up.

Dazed. Drugged. That's how he appears. His eyes blink slowly, then his lips move. An extremely satisfied grin appears. At least, I hope that's how he feels because that's sure how he looks. Unable to hold it in, I grin back. Maybe even beam.

I'm pretty damn proud of my accomplishment.

"I wasn't expecting that."

My lips slip together and I bite them. But not for long. I'm about to burst with pride, happiness and elation. My smile becomes all twisted as I try to fight it.

He pulls me against him with one arm as he quickly washes down the shower wall and floor before turning off the taps. "Lucky you have a big water tank."

I nod against his chest. He may have had the orgasm, but I'm the one fighting for words and breath. I've never done that. Never taken control. Never brought someone pleasure. Never made a man come. God, it was a completely heady experience.

"Are you okay?" he asks even though I'm sure they're the words I should say.

"I've never done that before."

His eyes widen and his brows shoot up. "You must have had lots of online practise, because that was sensational."

I chuckle. Do I say 'thank you'? What's the etiquette for sexual encounters? I decide to go with the same as any other situation. "Thanks. Sorry I went off script."

He snorts as he throws a towel towards me and grabs his own. "I'm not sorry for one moment." His grin warms me so much. "It'll mean I can give you my full and undivided attention...for a while anyway."

All that warmth cools. Not icy, so I must be improving. I didn't deliberately delay his fantasy. I'd acted on instinct, not even thinking about anal sex when I had my hand around his cock...

Oh my fucking god.

I look while the towel switches across his shoulder blades. My heart rate steadies. His cock isn't nearly as huge as the vision my mind just terrified me with. I take a couple of deep, slow breaths. I can do this. We've had two real sexual encounters and they've both been incredible. There's nothing to indicate the third will be a dud.

Two out of three ain't bad. The song lyrics came into my head complete with tune. Bloody mind. It's still trying to sabotage me.

My body, however, is listening to totally different music. My body and Seb's must be playing the same tune. Simultaneously, we reach for each other, fingers brushing before lacing together, effortlessly. We walk like that to my bedroom. Naked. Hands joined. Bodies speaking a language of their own.

I try to shut my mind off. It's annoying the heck out of me.

"It's okay that you're still nervous," Seb says as we

reach the side of my bed. "We could get dressed and go do something if you want?"

Right there. That's exactly why I shouldn't be scared. He reads me. Understands me. There's not one ounce of pressure. No man is more deserving of a completely mind-blowing fantasy.

"If I'm nervous, can we still do this? Is that okay?" My hesitance is horrid but I have to know if it's a turn off.

"Of course. If you weren't nervous about trying something new, I'd be worried." He holds my gaze. Truth. Leaning forwards, he touches his lips to mine. Softly. With such an aching tenderness I almost melt. "If you need to stop, say it, 'stop,' and I'll stop immediately. You don't have to do this."

He's right. I don't have to do this. I don't have to step outside my comfort zone. I don't have to do anything at all. But I want to.

I want to know what it's like. Anal sex, that is. Online, it gives me a buzz. The first time he spoke about it had been confronting, but then the taboo exploded and I became addicted to the thought of it.

If I'm honest with myself, his fantasy has become mine too. However, it's so difficult to admit that to myself, let alone say it out loud.

"I want to." His expression seems to soften and that gives me courage. "I want to know what your cock feels like as you break-in my arse." Honest to god, by the end of that sentence I'm whispering, but the look on his face is priceless. I've repeated words he's said online. He must realise as his pupils are huge, his mouth drops open, and his cock surges with blood. I don't get to check him out too much because he pulls me against him and his lips command mine. His tongue demands to explore my mouth.

He owns me now. Owns every part of my body. Owns every sexual beat that he drums from me. I'm his. Condamine has been claimed by Esquire...but there's no way on earth I'm admitting that out loud. It's my secret to keep.

His fingers slide down my belly and between my thighs. He lays me on the bed and my legs part, welcoming his touch. He fingers me—clit and vagina, labia and mons.

Then he tentatively touches my anus, glancing at me every few seconds checking I'm okay. His finger is gentle, but the effect is sky rockets. Fireworks. My body clenches hard. My brain tries to fight the giddy waves my body is sending. My brain is telling my legs to run, but my legs are lacking muscle control and they open further, giving Seb complete access.

He grabs the lube I've left, along with condoms, on my bedside table. I was hopeful, even if concerned. Health and safety are priorities for both of us. We've discussed that at some length online. Knowing his views on sexual health has countered some of the things I'd heard about men hating raincoats and refusing to wear them.

His hands rub together before he carefully dollops lube onto his finger. All this time, his gaze is trained on me, as if he's expecting me to chicken out, or run. But hell! I have a beautifully naked man, standing between my legs, cock so hard it's almost throbbing, and he's taking delicious care preparing me for what will no doubt be an experience more mind-blowing than I've imagined.

"Okay?" A slow smile makes his face light up with so much sweet and powerful energy, all I can do is stare and nod. When his eyebrows lift, I manage to murmur, "Yes. Ready."

He has a hand on my knee, gently holding my legs. He places a pillow, tipping my hips for easier access, just like he said online. I'm watching, almost without blinking, because this is surreal. He may vanish and I might waken from this incredibly erotic dream to find myself sitting at the computer. It's nothing like the same experience, and yet, there are so many similarities.

Lube glistens on his fingers as he squeezes the tube. Air catches in my chest. *We're really doing this.* I'm exposed. Completely. He's almost a stranger. *Damn my brain.* That snagged breath seems to be holding back panic. There could be a stampede of innards. It's all going to come spilling out. As my mouth opens to release mayhem, I catch his gaze, full of care and concern. That stare seems to reach inside and settle all the panic down. Air releases and my indrawn breath flows clear. Seb's eyes widen and I answer with a nod and a smile that hopefully looks confident.

We're in this together.

Unable to draw my gaze from his face, I have peripheral vision of his lubed fingers disappearing from sight. His gaze is intense as he's looking at my body, his eyes lift to mine for a second, and the cold pressure lands slap bang in the middle of my anus. Every part of me sucks inward. Air fills my lungs but gets stuck as all the muscles from below tense and hurtle upwards. My toes clench into the bedsheets. It's not panic this time.

"Sorry, it's too cold. I thought my finger would heat it."

I shake my head. It's the shock, not the temperature. But those words are never going to come. Everything's still balled in my middle, and not one muscle has relaxed enough for tasks like speaking or breathing.

The tube of lube rests on my stomach and he squeezes a small pool onto my flesh. There's another sharp squeeze of muscle, and a puff of air pops from between my lips. "That will warm it." He dips his fingertips into the liquid, swirling it across my skin, before his fingers drag the liquid over my mons and between my labia. Wet. Soft pads of his fingers rub against my clit.

It's magic. Every muscle magically eases and a moan follows. "Easy, easy," he murmurs as he slides more lube across my clit. I should be able to tell him that it's good now. That my body's relaxing and easing and feeling more comfortable, even while exposed, but my brain seems to have lost the battle and retired. No speech is possible. It's difficult enough to make sounds, let alone words.

Another lube-coated finger skims my vagina before circling my anus and I'm not sure what to do. Half of me tries to clench, but my clit is sending all these, 'oh my god, this is so good,' messages. I'm like an undulating wave, half relaxing then tensing, depending on which finger is sending the strongest signal to my overwhelmed mind.

I have never felt so bloody amazing.

When my anus gets accustomed to the sensation of his finger circling, he begins to press against it. A momentary clench, but when there's no penetration, tension releases and absolute bliss threads through me. I'm so incredibly caught up in the swirling, circling that I think I may have melted into the bed.

A deep slow breath fills my lungs. My eyes drift closed.

His finger slips into me.

Fuck.

Fuck. Fuck. Fuck.

So fucking tight.

He's saying stuff, and his other hand is on my clit, then rubbing against my vagina walls, sliding over my labia, but there's not enough feeling from any of that to override the shock. My entire focus is on clenching my arse and keeping out the intruder.

Short sharp breaths hurt. Trying to squirm hurts. I lay still. Frozen.

After a few dramatic, panic-stretched seconds, my breath comes again. I can squirm without discomfort. My clit throbs beneath his expert touch. My back relaxes, maybe even stretches, arches.

I focus on his voice. He's steadying me, asking me to breathe, questioning if I want him to stop. There's no panic in his tone, just warmth. Sweet, gentle warmth that soothes.

I don't want this to stop. No way. Somewhere amongst that shock and ache there's the tiniest feeling of excitement. A tingle of something more than intrigue. "Don't stop," I manage to stammer.

He chuckles and pinches my clit between thumb and forefinger. *Oh yeah. Oh yeah.* I soak up every bit of that pleasure, pressing into his touch, drowning in bliss.

And then, another sharp rocket of hurt. I gasp. Breath lodges. My clit pounds. It doesn't want this clenching reaction; it needs breath, movement, relaxation. I consciously take a breath and relax, just a tad. Pain flees.

I ease against the bedsheets, and there's not even a twinge of an ache.

His fingers slip from my clit to my vagina, gently pushing inside again. Soft, gentle, full. "Do it now," I gasp, hoping he'll know what I mean.

He slides the other finger deeper into my arse, and the moment I tense, his finger stops. Not those in my vag, they kept on rubbing and probing and sending me all the delicious sensations. "Oh yeah." I manage to get those out as words, breathy and probably indecipherable, but at least they're not jammed in my head.

He sets up some movement that turns me to a molten mess. His fingers move over labia, clit and inside my vagina, constantly sending the most tantalising messages all over my body. I don't know whether to push or tuck, moan or gasp.

"Ease up, Caitlyn. I'm going to try to insert my second finger. Just breathe like you have been. You're doing so well. Your arse is so fucking tight, it's beautiful."

Two fingers? Fuck. That's only one? I glance at my hand clawing at the bedsheets. Fingers aren't anywhere near as big as his stiff cock. Nerves jitter. Muscles tense tighter.

I blink slowly, trying to fight the urge to ask him to

stop. Not with both hands, just the one that's pushing in a foreign place. The one that's asking for access where access hasn't been granted before. My eyes spring wide and I yelp. A sting shoots through. Confused, I look down to my leg, which seems to be the centre of the smarting, and his head is against my inner thigh, his tongue lapping, easing the sharp sting of his nip.

As the ache in my thigh eases, I become conscious of a tight stretch in my arse but almost as soon as I recognise it, pleasure pounding from my clit overrides everything.

His gaze ensnares mine. Without letting go, he leans forward, tongue outstretched, and licks along my inner thigh. My whole body quivers. It's completely delicious. Especially when he laps right across the red he's marked me with. He could be a huge, completely satisfied cat.

Before I have any more coherent thought, he plays my body again. My novice cells react to his exquisite music, humming. Body moving as his hand conducts. My cunt aches. Clit throbs. Arse not quite sure how it's feeling, sometimes trumpeting sharply, other times immersed in the pleasure symphony with the other parts.

Holy fuck. It's magnificent. He looks as intently at me as he does at my body. I'm exposed and examined, and that, incredibly, makes me needier. I want to open further for him. I want him to read me completely, see me fully, so he can create more of this exquisite concert.

His fingers stretch and open me. They dance over sensitive flesh, heightening my arousal. I've never felt this high, this lost. I want to crash into oblivion, even as I want this to continue for eternity.

"It's easier if I roll you over to enter you." I hear the

words, he even carefully rolls me over so I'm on my stomach and no longer lost in his gaze. He lifts me, positions me, and I'm like a liquid spilling to wherever he points me.

"Ready?"

"Yes. Yes." The words mindlessly spill. I'm ready for eternity or oblivion, or both together.

His fingers clasp my hip and I wish they were pinching my clit. As I make that wish, my clit pulses, throbbing as if his touch is there.

There's pressure on my arse again. I know this. This tightness, the pinch of clenching that gives way to blissful filling. When his fingers pinch my clit, I won't even think of his fingers stretching my arse, invading my body in such a way that it messes with my mind.

"Breathe," he says and I obey. "Push back against me, don't fight this. Keep breathing." The words fill me with the deep longing his voice inspires. The longing for bliss, fulfilment...

Holy fuck.

That clenching from before was nothing compared with this. I'm clamped tight as something huge probes my arse.

"Easy, baby. Push out and breathe. Relax." All these words. Instructions. I can't follow. I can't think. I'm focussed on pain. Hurt. Stinging. Tight. Tension.

Hand between my legs, stroking me, my clit. Pain decreasing. Muscles relaxing. Breath happening. I can draw in air. I push back.

Fuck. Fuckity fuck fuck.

Sharp gasps are all I can manage.

What am I doing? What the hell is he doing? I can't do...

Oh.

One long spasm ripples through.

Yes.

"That's it. That's it. You're taking me." His fingers strum my clit in time with his words, like a reward. "Deep breaths. Relax. That's good." My body seems to be doing what he's saying. All my focus is on the way he's rolling my clit and the shudders of pleasure he's drawing out of me.

"I'm buried in your arse and it's amazing. You're so tight. So beautifully tight." Those words register. The 'buried in your arse' is what he says when his cyber-cock is deep in me during cyber-sex, but it never felt like this. Like I'm filled, stretched, not sure if I should move or not. The act of breathing is something I'm thinking carefully about rather than naturally doing.

"Keep breathing. That's it." With one hand still commanding a response from my clit, his other is on my spine, that super-sensitive bit right at the base, stroking, circling, soothing.

I'm going to purr. As my back dips, he moves. I freeze solid. I want to scream, "No," at the same time as I want his cock out of this foreign space. As his cock withdraws, I don't want it to go. There's some intense loss I don't understand. I whimper.

"Easy. I'm going to fuck you now. Keep breathing. It shouldn't hurt any more. It should just get better."

If I had a few coherent thoughts I might scoff, or even argue. As it is, I breathe and that's difficult enough. That remnant of pain has a hold on my body and it's not letting go even as the slide of his cock distracts me.

Then he pushes inside me. The slap of his flesh on mine assures me he's buried deep, and there is no pain.

There is no pain.

Rapid breathing happens almost instantaneously. Ripples race through my body. Words spill from me. Incoherent words of encouragement, to fuck me, fill me, go harder, faster, deeper. More. It's so good.

It's so amazingly good.

He moves, and I move.

I can't get enough. I want him thrusting hard. Harder. Filling me totally. Completely.

It's so animalistic. A deep musky scent fills the air. His hand moves, his cock moves. I'm dripping, drowning. He's faster. His cock is pummelling me. Speed. Sensation. Depth. So much fucking depth. Or width. Is it width not depth that's stretching, filling, pushing me beyond any other experience?

I need. Want. I'm fucking bursting to come.

Please. Please. Please. Begging. For what? Faster? Harder? Continuation? Release?

Clit. Pulsing. Arse. Taut. Tightening. Loosening. He thrusts more before he cries out. My anal ring tightens around his pounding cock and explosion. An animal screams loudly.

Me. Him.

Who the fuck knows?

My collapse leads to being sprawled flat on the bed which suggests that I've exploded. That my orgasm has taken everything from me. Every skerrick of control.

Unable to hold my body up, or open my eyes. I'm panting but can't move my mouth, so it's probably locked open, after that animal scream, without the ability to close.

Prickles itch across my eyes and I can't even manage to blink away those tears of release. I let them spill in time to the rapid drum of my heart.

There hasn't been a lot of sex in my life but if I never manage to have sex again, I could survive on the memory of these encounters.

And he's here for a few more days. I bet if my mouth could move, my smile would be one of total and complete wickedness. He is not leaving this house. I need more sex. More anal sex.

I will never be able to have enough mind-blowing sex like this.

"You okay?" His voice is a rasp as his lips brush against the edge of my ear.

"More than." A few huffs before those words form but his sinful chuckle made the effort worthwhile.

"Breathe and relax as I pull out, okay?" I whimper a protest but he's already sliding free of me. As his cock pops free, it's as if he's taken a part of me with him. I'm empty. Raw and empty. "God, you're gaping." He sounds incredulous, while I feel as if I'll never go back to how I was before. My life will never be the same. He has a place inside me.

Not my heart, but fuck, it's much more intimate.

While I'm pulling pieces of myself together, he cleans up, cleans me up, gently with warm wet care. Then he curls against me and holds me. Helping me pull all the pieces of me back together. As he touches and strokes, his words are a balm gluing me back together.

"Your arse was so tight." "That was so good." "Better than I dreamed." "Thank you for sharing with me." "God, you were tight." "That arse..." "So tight."

When I'm no longer fragile, I meet his gaze and I lose myself in the raw honesty I can see. I was going to ask how it really was for him, but I don't need to. I can see. His words aren't a superficial balm aimed to please me. "Would you like to do that again some time?"

His lips move a tiny bit. For a moment, I think he's going to laugh, and don't think I'm strong enough for him to joke... or decline. A momentary pang of regret hits me. I glance away.

His hand slides across my body, slips beneath my chin and makes me meet his gaze. "Yes. Thank you." That perfectly polite response makes my body sing. A smile erupts from my very core and seems to be echoed in the one he shares with me. "I'd love to do that again... except I'm incapable right this moment."

And doesn't that make me feel like preening, if only I had the energy. Wrapped around each other, with huge smiles, I relax as I never have before. Safe. Secure. So very ready for whatever sexual pleasure we're next to share.

In my mind, I see ESQUIRE SIGNS OUT but I mentally adjust that, because neither of us are signing out right now. We're here, together, and there's no place I'd rather be.

Thank you for reading A Real Online Fantasy Parts
1 & 2

I really appreciate the time you've given to read Caitlyn and Seb's story. I hope you enjoyed it.

I'm thinking about writing further adventures of their online and real fantasies, so if you enjoyed this, keep a lookout for new stories. You could always join my Mailing List and I'll drop you an email when I have a new books out. I won't send many emails, I'm not big on newsletters.

BONUS CONTENT

I've included the short stories from the anthologies edited by Rachel Kramer Bussel and Rose Caraway. If you enjoy these short stories, please consider buying the anthologies. They've been out for a while now and they're packed full of all sorts of interesting stories. Available in print, ebook and audio (narrated by Rose Caraway).

PAIN SURFER

From *Gotta Have It: 69 Stories of Sudden Sex*. Edited by
Rachel Kramer Bussel.

The beach is deserted on this cold, wet Sunday
and it matches my mood. Waves roll
continuously, rhythmically pounding against the wet
sand. I walk along the tide line, feeling the water caress
my feet with the ebb and flow of the surf. I am headed
towards the rocks at the end of the beach. It's somewhere
to go.

There's a man trying to win control over the oceans
fury. I watch him surf as I walk towards the rocks. Maybe
it's something about his manner, his fierce attack of the
waves, that catches my eye. He seems driven to control
and it excites me in a very primitive way. I am shaken to
the core. My insides churn at the thought of being

controlled by such a man – is it excitement or terror? I'm not sure. I want to flee but feel compelled to stay. With each step I feel heat crawl down my thighs and through my body until I am burning.

I sit on the rocks to watch him exert his power over Neptune, God of the Sea. The struggle is exhilarating. It's not only the movement of his body as muscles press against the sleek black of the wetsuit but also the flip and dive of the board as it conquers and rides across waves. I am mesmerised by the dance. I sit motionless, almost in a trance, as I allow the rhythm of ocean and man to dominate my mind and body.

He rides a wave straight towards me. The breath jams in my throat. He's so close to the rocks. His smile dazzles me and I realise he has deliberately confronted death to scare me. He twists off the back of the wave and drops into the trough of sea. Relief is instant. I had thought he would be injured, torn from the ocean and shredded on rocks.

I sigh and stand, ready to leave. The spell is now broken. Before I take a step, I spy him climbing from the surf and walking towards me. His body fills the wetsuit as if it's a second skin. Muscles ripple leaving nothing to my imagination. My stomach flips slowly and tightens with primordial need. My gaze fixes on the protrusion of his cock. With great difficulty, and a furious blush, I draw my eyes to the rest of his physique.

Sinfully muscular thighs extend to powerful calves and long, wide feet. A flat stomach rises to a wide chest and square shoulders. His hair is slicked back, shaggy and dark blonde. His face is tanned and his lips generous even though pulled into another dazzling smile. A dimple flashes in his left cheek. His chin is deeply grooved. His eyes are the colour of the ocean in a storm and just as intense and possibly dangerous. They hold my gaze when I meet them.

He puts his board down, away from the pull of the ocean, and comes closer. Still I don't move. My mouth is open as I stare. I hope I'm not gaping but I can taste the ocean in the air as it caresses my tongue.

His cool, wet, strong hands lift towards my face before he cups my cheeks and dips until his lips meet mine. He tastes of salt, sea and fury. I cannot move. The kiss sears my lips. Heat floods my body. I meet the power of his kiss. I devour his lips as he attacks mine. I explore his mouth as he plunders mine. My hands tour his body, learning his shape and feel, running over wetsuit-clad muscles that bunch beneath my touch.

It isn't enough. I need flesh. I have to feel heat, the heat from taut muscles, skin. I pull on the zipper at the back of his wetsuit. I can't break the kiss. I need his taste. I hear the squelch as the wetsuit pulls away from wet shoulder blades. I peel the wetsuit forwards. My hands fumble as the heat of his flesh hits my palms. His mouth still plunders mine and I am caught in the kiss and flounder as I feel the heat of his flesh. Finally powerful shoulders then sleek chest break free. The wetsuit falls to bunch between us.

My fingers and palms rub, touch, pinch and tease his chest and shoulders. We never break the kiss. The kiss holds such power it makes the surf seem calm. Lips search, devour, taste, nibble. Teeth nip, bite, graze. Tongues dance, circle, duel, stroke.

Nothing can maintain this intensity and slowly the kiss gentles. Now the need to touch consumes me. My hands burn against his body. His hands dance over my skin. He cups my breasts, soothes over my hips, strokes across my stomach and eases down my thighs. A trail of fire. He is everywhere and yet I need more. I can't feel enough of him. I drag the wetsuit lower, push it over his hips and bottom, skin it down his legs. We struggle until I remember - zips at ankles. I'm surprised my mind is that active. I shed him of his wetsuit and admire his proud, tanned body.

His cock already stands proud, drawing me closer. He laughs a deep throaty sound as my hand curls into a fist around his cock and I tug him against me. Our mouths again meet in fierce combat. My naked breasts hit his damp chest. When did he undress me? All I felt was his touch.

As our mouths duel, my hand strokes his cock until it pulses against my palm. It holds an awesome power in itself, waiting to be unleashed. It is as rigid as every muscle in his toned body. I curl my leg around his and thrust my hips forward. I want his solid cock inside me. I need to feel his power surging upwards.

His throaty laugh as he pulls away sends shudders straight to my bursting cunt. He knows how badly I need him. He takes my hand and leads me to a large, flat rock, like a cliff face. He presses himself, standing, against it and I climb him, using his shoulders to hold myself as I angle and spear myself onto his shaft. As I sink, I gasp. *Fuck, is it that big?* I pant as my body screams. Muscles stretch trying to accommodate him. I lift my head, pull my body backwards, pulling off his cock until I feel the cool salty air hit my heated cunt.

He grins but holds my hips tight, fingers pressing into my flesh. He leans forward and sucks my nipple into his heated mouth. I groan in pleasure as moisture pools and again I sink onto his cock, writhing with need. He fills me to breaking. His cock pulses within. I don't know if I can move. Time stands suspended. I ache with pain and pleasure, unsure which is going to win. Can I bear the pain of his cock filling me? I am struggling ... and then he bites my lip. Not a nip but a deep bite. Shock holds me still.

Pain draws my focus to my lip and frees my mind from the pain in my cunt. His cock twitches and I move. Pleasure fills me. My hips follow the pounding rhythm of the surf. I rise and fall on his cock. I'm the ebb and flow of the tide. Movement is slow until the pounding of the waves inside my head are louder than the ocean and I take my rhythm from my internal need.

I am mesmerised by his eyes, watching them darken with pleasure as we fuck. I know we're both close. I can feel the tension. My body screams for release but I can't find it. I ache to let go. I throb. My body is caught in the high but unable to snap from it and find my release. I make a tormented, guttural, frustrated scream.

He shifts his weight. He over-balances and we're

toppling. I guess my scream shocked him. He holds me tight but he can't protect me. We hit the ground. A rock stabs into my thigh and I feel the jaggered tear of stone ripping flesh. My body bucks as pain surrounds me. Blackness threatens to consume me. I draw deep gasping breaths and fight the consuming darkness.

And then I feel it. The rhythm, the ocean, his cock. Movement, ancient rhythms, inside me. The shock of pain blurs. My mind is lost. The pain releases me from myself. I scream as ecstasy fills me. I rear beneath him. My hips arch and my cunt squeezes and pulses around his cock. He thrusts and quivers as his release hits. Hot seed shoots into me.

I writhe. Bite his shoulder as my body tears apart, as if each cell is torn from another. My cunt milks him as my orgasm hits. My cunt curls around his cock as if never to release him. My clit bursts. Colours, bright and dark, fill my mind. The surging crescendo screams a perfect long note. My body is a million shattered pieces.

I feel the sting of hot tears course down my cheeks. I hold him tight because it's all I can do to keep myself together. I feel the heat of cum and cunt juice trail my thighs. I feel the biting pain of rock against flesh.

Then I feel the gentle brush of thumb pad against cheek bone. I smile. The storm tossed seas smile back at me. He doesn't need to ask, he knows how damn good that was, it's etched on my face. He holds me until I can feel each piece of my body pull together again. He kisses me softly as his cock withdraws and I shudder as if a vital part of _my_ body is withdrawn. I know it's his, but it belonged in me. My breath slows and he pulls me up until I stand before him. He touches his lips against my nose and turns to leave. I watch him go, back to tame the angry sea.

The End

CONTROL

From *The Big Book of Submission: 69 Kinky Tales.*
Edited by Rachel Kramer Bussel

"Visitors at eight, pet." His soft words, laced with command, make my body thrum.

Dashiell Traversham is forty, well-to-do, and not unattractive, but the attributes I adore are his domination, quiet demands and disciplines. He makes my cunt weep and my eyes run. He fills my holes with his seed and I love him more with each drop expelled. When he enters a room, it shrinks, filled with his scents of sandalwood and the sea. I don't need to see to know him. I know every lithe muscle. Every dark hair. Every stretch of tanned flesh. How he tastes. How he likes to be touched.

Dashiell's words may sound like he's letting me know his plans but this is what I hear. "By seven-thirty tonight you need to be completely denuded of hair, except for your head—that hair will be washed and scented, brushed until it's burnished gold. Refreshments need to be prepared and left ready to be served. You're to present yourself to the study at seven-thirty, and without a word to or from me, bend over the padded metal frame until your cunt is exposed like artwork, to be admired by my visitors. You may or may not be touched; you have no say in that. You are to remain silent and immobile until I ask you, by name, to act in another manner."

I spend the day preparing. Tiny petit fours, delicate sandwiches, decadent peppermint molded chocolates set out. My skin exfoliated until it shines. The bar fully stocked. Every hair removed. Coffee ground and percolated. Flexibility exercises complete. Study dusted and tidied until spotless. Hair brushed with three hundred strokes.

By seven-thirty my cunt is swollen, my clit tender with anticipation. I knock once on the heavy wood of the closed study door. At his command, I enter and walk to the padded bar. It bends me exactly in half, taking my weight when my feet no longer can. The thick padded leather cushions ensure there's no discomfort.

Stiletto-clad feet spread apart, I drape myself across the bar and bend forward. I feel Dashiell watching. My flexibility has increased since the last visitors. I bend in half fluidly.

The leather against my hips and stomach is cool. The burn in the back of my legs increases as I lower my head. A cascade of hair smothers the wooden boards. Heavy breasts strain as I swing forward, dropping toward my lowered head, stretching the flesh across my ribs. My nipples squeeze. Blood rushes to my brain in a pounding rush. When I first tried this, I orgasmed from the rush of blood, but I've learned control. I wonder if Dashiell remembers.

His cane was so quick back then. I earned it often. An orgasm followed by the cane equaled a double coming. Punishment and reward.

My cunt weeps as Dashiell glances at me. He's a man well-pleased, which makes my juices seep.

The next thirty minutes are the hardest. I want his touch, yet he's working. I'm desperate for his soothing words, curious as to who's coming, and curiosity always makes me gush.

Finally, the doorbell sounds and Dashiell rises. He walks past me without a touch and inside I whimper. I'd hoped for a brush of his fingers across my cunt, or a slip of his nail along my open lips, or perhaps the lap of his tongue against my clit.

Nothing.

Voices. They enter. A woman I don't know and Dashiell. The woman strides across the room, heels rapping on the boards, and stares at me as if I am an object d'art. Only the faintest caress of breath lets me know she's inspecting my cunt. My hole opens as if to stare back at her. Moisture trickles. I worry I'm not pleasing her, not pleasing Dashiell. I want to weep. What if she finds fault?

She has covered shoes with towering, thin heels. The patent leather shines. I try not to breathe and fog them. Her shapely legs are encased in dark smoke hose; a black dress skims beneath her knees. I'd only glimpsed her walking in; pale flesh, black hair, black dress, red lipstick.

"Of course." Dashiell answers a question I have not heard. Muscles inside me tense, waiting. What has been asked? What must I do?

A crisp floral perfume weaves itself around me but before I can luxuriate in her scent, she strokes the inside of my thigh with her fingernail. Her gasp sucks air across my lips, so I know she's leaning, examining closely. My cunt clenches as I try not to squirm. The thick warmth of her breath brushes over my anus. She's staring intently at my hole. It pulls tight in protest. But a breeze blown hard on my clit has my body jerking, both holes relaxing, and a wetness seeping through me. I shudder despite myself, losing the fight to remain still, to keep my reactions internal.

Footsteps patter across the room but they're background noise. I'm focused on my task. A whoosh and my attention is brought abruptly back. My cunt clenches just as the bamboo cane strikes across it, hard. I cry out. Pain, shock, and a tiny fission of pleasure rip through me. My clit throbs. Nipples tighten. I bite back any other sound or reaction. *Oh dear lord.* Dashiell hasn't caned my open lips in so long. The sting pounds through my body, setting it on fire. My hole opens and closes, like my mouth wants to, weeping the tears I cannot.

A strong smell of candle wax comes to my attention just as a plop hits my anus. At first there's nothing; it lasts but a millisecond. Then the scalding burn forces the breath from me. A scream echoes in my head. A scream not just of pain but of pleasure too. My clit throbs until I think it may burst. The pain vanishes as quickly as the wax dries. Only tension, in every tightly wound muscle of my body, remains.

"How exquisite." The woman's voice is breathy and husky. The flick of her nail along my cunt lips almost has me twitching, but I stop myself. The nail—I imagine it long and gleaming red—picks the wax droplet from my anus. Spasms hit. Another mini-orgasm. I almost melt into the padded bench.

"She holds herself well, Dashiell." The woman's voice softens as she walks away from me. I hear snatches of her conversation. "A credit to you...I'd like to show her..." I can't put the words together. My head is spinning with rapture, trying to fight not only the physical sensations she's elicited from me, but the mental ones too. The sheer joy of knowing I've succeeded, knowing I'll be rewarded, knowing I've pleased, is more powerful than the cane, wax and tongue put together. I'm almost unconscious trying to fight the sweeping orgasm threatening me.

But I must wait.

Eyes scrunched in concentration, I count each breath until my body is under control. Under Dashiell's control.

The End

~

MICHAELS'S MOMENT

From *Tonight, She's Yours: Cuckold Fantasies*. Edited by
Rose Caraway.

The sip of wine lies heavily on my tastebuds.
I'm hoping a glass of wine in the hotel bar will
kill time while relaxing me. It's not doing well yet. I wish
I'd ordered a light sparkling but I thought there were
enough bubbles inside me without adding to them.

With my fingernail I chase a droplet of water from
the bowl down the stem to the base. One deep inhalation.
Hold. Exhale slowly.

One small sip. Put the glass down.

I resist a large swallow, like I resisted ordering
sparkling wine, or shots of tequila. I even refrain from
tapping a rhythm on the edge of the bar with my
fingernails by curling my hands into fists. Such restraint.

Have you ever been on a blind date?

This is worse.

My stomach churns. And it's not the wine. It's been tumbling and twisting for hours.

It's not only because I'm meeting someone new. It's also because this "date" is supposed to be perfect for me, just what I want, gorgeous, suited, et cetera.

What if he isn't perfect?

Another sip that doesn't settle me. It takes me out of my mind, though, for a few seconds. Longer if I chase another water droplet. Longer again if I look around the bar. It's not crowded so there's not a lot to capture my attention.

I'm waiting for my husband, and the lover he's chosen for me.

Insane, right?

This has the potential for disaster. Although, maybe I'm pessimistic. Michael would say I am. Michael's my husband. The man I love. The man I chose to share my life with. Tonight I'm cheating on him, while he watches.

It's Michael's fantasy. His deepest desire, burning need, aching want. I've tried to talk him out of it for years, without success. He's adamant he wants to watch me being fucked, and not by just anyone. He's chosen this guy not just as the perfect fuck for me but as someone better than him. That's a lot of pressure to put on a guy, not that Michael is likely to tell him. But I'm going to be judging him, Michael's going to be judging him, and it won't be easy. Although he is a professional. Michael found that reassuring.

One night stands can be so bloody awkward. All that

raging lust can fizzle into nothing once the sex gets real. And that's without an audience.

Shit. What am I doing?

What if there's no chemistry? What if I can't get interested? What if the guy can't fuck me good enough? What if—

Holy fuck.

My mouth drops open and the warm air moving in steals every drop of moisture—or else every droplet just roared south.

Michael's walking towards me, but it's not him that makes me gasp. After waking next to him for twenty years my gasps have expired. Or I thought they had until the guy stalking beside Michael made me shut up and notice.

Norse God. Viking.

He doesn't walk. Nothing so mundane. There's something animalistic in his movements. Raw and hedonistic. Smooth and supple. Lean and long-legged. His muscles ripple.

I blink. Again.

He's fully clothed. How the hell do I know his muscles ripple? Where is my brain? Lust has taken over. The knots have begun to unravel.

Initial chemistry is present. I'd fuck this guy. I'd dance with him, against him, on top of him. Fuck. I'd forget my husband for him. Michael? Who's he? Is he that older guy who keeps trying to push in on me and the hot Viking?

Except Michael won't push in. Michael will watch but not participate. Not even to touch me.

And that's not the worst.

Michael wants me to humiliate him even further. I have to compare Michael's prowess against that of the man we're paying to screw me. I have to tell Michael how much bigger the guy is, how much better he feels inside, how much more his touch gives, and why my orgasm is better from this stud.

I haven't found anyone better in all these years...but this guy. *This guy.*

"Janice, this is Emil." Michael's voice has a breathlessness I haven't heard before. In all the fantasies we've enacted, he's never been this aroused. His pupils have dilated so that his usually brown eyes are almost black. His lips don't seem to be capable of remaining closed. The tip of his tongue runs along his lower lip, then against his upper, back to his lower. It's gone. Then pokes at the other side, a flick of movement, a dart of pink. But I can't watch Michael, I have Emil to meet... and screw.

"Jan-ice." I've never heard my name like that. So goddamn sexy. My legs get watery. He's put a deep weight on the first part of my name like he's thrusting into me, then an exhale at the end, as if he loves being buried deep inside.

I glance up, intending to reply, but instead I drown in arctic blue eyes as timeless as a glacier. Perfect for his blonde, strong Nordic features and aloofness.

His blink releases me. It's not that millisecond blink Michael does, it's a blink that takes a millennia. Thick lashes lower until the ice is covered and lashes interlace. The skin on his eyelids appears soft and smooth. I'd like to lick it, softly, as a butterfly tastes nectar.

A not-so-discreet clearing of the throat breaks my insane daydream and I stumble over his name. My mind functioning at about one one hundredth of normal speed, if that. I drag my lips into what hopefully resembles a polite smile and try again. "Emil, nice to meet you."

His nose is stronger than Michael's, as is his jaw. Bone structure more prominent. I think about rival males in nature and wonder if Emil's face would give him more fighting prowess, an advantage when looking for a mate. Is this something Michael considered when evaluating this man?

For all that harsh bone structure, there's softness too. Perfectly blended. Arctic eyes, cliff-like bones, pink-flushed cheeks, sinful lips and blonde curls long enough to lose my hands in, shouldn't go together. But they do. So help me, they do.

"Shall we have a drink, dinner?" Michael asks.

I couldn't swallow a thing, except maybe... One look down and my throat constricts while my mouth waters. Emil's erect cock pushes against his jeans as if wanting to be swallowed. I could take that. I could take his cock deep into my throat, gagging and choking on that width, the barely constrained length. The sweetness of his pre-cum would fill my mouth with—

Michael's hand squeezes my shoulder, slides down my back. I take a step away from his hand and towards Emil as Emil responds, "Not for me, thanks."

What does he mean? Is that some code for bailing out because he can't fuck me?

My heart skips a beat.

But a turn of my head shows Michael's tiniest hint of jealousy. His eyes have narrowed, lips pursed, jaw ticking. Emil wants me. What he doesn't want is drinks or dinner.

He wants me.

That makes me giddy. I suspect Michael's a little less pleased about it.

That shouldn't excite me.

Oh, God. The bit I thought would be the most difficult, is turning out to give me nasty satisfaction. Teenage Janice is enjoying two men sparring over her. Not that there's any sparring... I'm riding high on the feeling of invincibility, control and utter desirousness as the two men circle me.

"I'm right." My voice is strong, secure and sexy. Michael blinks, rocks back before recovering and nodding. I've protested quite a bit about this fantasy, he's probably more shocked than I at how this is going. Although he's always maintained that I'd love it, that I'd be so into it, that he'd have me begging for more. There's something about Emil that suggests this might be true.

Michael booked a room for the weekend, so we make our way from the bar to the room. I want to say it's awkward but there's something non-awkward about it too. I wonder if it's sort of a mission-based awkwardness. We're focussed on what's ahead, so lust swirls masking any other feeling any of us may have. This is mob mentality with lust instead of anger or fear.

Michael's hand shakes as he tries to swipe the room card. I give him two attempts before I mould my body around him, extend my hand over his and take control. The green light flicks and the door clicks unlocked.

We enter and something happens.

My control slips. All the confidence I had when I opened that door, vanishes in a moment. What am I doing? What are *we* doing?

Michael's hand slides along my spine and little bursts of energy spark from his touch. His nose nestles against my ear, his warmth fills me where I have none. The tip of his tongue traces the edge of my earlobe and I shudder, pressing my butt against his rigid cock as I always do. Instinct driving me to comfort.

'You right, Jan?" There's just the thread of tension in that whispered question. His abbreviation of my name is unusual. He does that only at the peak of arousal.

I shake my head hoping he can feel the movement. I don't mind Michael seeing, he knows my every fear. I don't want Emil to see my hesitance, although his back is turned while he examines the view. Or maybe he's polite enough, or experienced enough, to give us a moment.

"He's hot for you, babe." Michael's soft voice in my ear has me focussing on pleasure. I love the heat as his breath caresses the sensitive skin. His words are unexpected but exactly what I need to hear from him. "His huge dick was straining for your pussy. Did you see that? And his eyes have been fucking you since he saw you. He wants you." His tongue slides, wet and hot, at the back of my ear and deep shudders fill me. "He's going to fuck you hard, harder than I can. He's going to fill you with his spunk. Come all over your gorgeous big tits. Fuck you over and over until you can think of nothing but coming harder and harder each time." He's got me so hot now. His tongue toys wickedly with my ear and neck. His words are killing me. "He's young. His cock won't wear out. He'll be fucking you all night and I know you'll love every second of it. And I'll be watching you. I'll know that you're loving it." I should hear jealousy or fear in his voice but it's not there. His voice is thready, breathy, full of need. "You're going to tell me, aren't you? You're going to tell me how much you're enjoying his big thick hard cock."

Oh. God.

I can almost feel a huge cock pushing into me. He has me soaked, horny and so very very wet.

It's his cock as well as his words and mouth. With every sentence his cock gets harder, thicker, stronger. Rubbing against my arse, he's getting off on telling me what will happen. He wants this. He wants this so much more than I ever understood. I can do this for him. Anything for him. And Emil... Michael knows my type better than I do.

"Emil?" Michael waits for Emil to turn then he presents me to him. "Janice is yours for the rest of the evening." He gives me a little push forwards so there's no longer contact between us, or maybe he steps backwards, I don't know. I'm jumbled up inside. Michael's voice catches but he keeps speaking. "I...I know you'll look... after her." He struggles to get those last words out but I can't turn to reassure or comfort him. I have been passed to Emil and he's taken my hands in his, his touch light but commanding.

"I promise to treat her well." Emil's voice. *Damn it*

all. Dark chocolate is positively saintly compared with the richness of his voice. It rushes down my spine, lingers on my fingertips, and dances across my toes.

Reality's gone. Replaced by lust. Sexy, seductive and sinful.

Emil holds me gently, watching me closely. Then his thumb slides across my palm and electricty shoots through. Bolts of lightning, shocking me from my indecision.

Want. Need.

Without taking my hands from his, I step towards him, stand on my tip toes and lick along the open vee of his t-shirt. He tastes better than I dreamed. Tangy, like an ocean spray, and smoky, like a barbeque, with hints of rich spiciness. Before I can taste further, one hand disengages from mine and slides beneath my chin. He doesn't push my chin up, it's more coaxed, and I meet his gaze for a second before his mouth touches mine.

Lightning bolt to wildfire.

His lips devour mine. They're more generous than Michael's in size and in ability. The brief caress when our lips met quickly becomes an inferno. No time for getting to know each other. No gentleness. Just devastating devouring.

I love it.

I haven't felt this in over twenty years. The complete annihilation of inhibition. Where clothes are shred from bodies without thought. Without stepping apart. Without the kiss breaking.

Heady madness.

Complete insanity.

Fuck, I need him.

Now.

Clawing at his chest and shoulders I'm as effective as a kitten against a wooden door. He doesn't move. He's controlled and I'm so far from control I forget what it means. While I'm still grasping at him trying to make him take me quickly, as I do with Michael, he's jammed one solid thigh between my legs.

His fingers dig into my hips and he rocks me. A thought hits. I could come on his thigh. I want his cock, but I could come like this. Just like this.

His lips still wreck mine as his hands slide over my ribs from my hips. My body trembles, waiting, wanting. I want those big calloused hands on my breasts. His hands will cover them. I want them there. Need them there. Already I feel them so close.

Then his hands stop. I growl into his mouth, wanting to beg him to touch my boobs but before I can utter a word, his tongue invades my space.

Fuck me.

His taste.

God.

His taste is...

Oh.

Squirming on his leg, his tongue fucks my mouth while he twists each nipple in opposite directions until I'm going to explode.

Or scream.

Or tear apart.

Panting for breath, I can't make sense of my body. It's never been like this. How can I be ready so damn fast?

His lips pull away and air bursts into my mouth, my lungs, my brain. I manage to drag a hand free, levering my nails out of his clenched shoulder muscle. I want to catch his cock but my arms are stuck up near his shoulders so I snatch a fistful of his hair instead.

Angling his head back to mine, I capture his nose, suck along the boney ridge before dropping to his mouth.

Jesus. I sucked his nose?

His lips. *God.* Touching them is like...dessert. A gooey, soft, sweet deliciousness that I can't eat quickly enough even though I want to savour it.

While I'm kissing him until my brain melts, his fingers keep tweaking my nipples until I can feel them pounding more strongly than my clit rubbing along his hairy thigh. I never thought my clit could be drowned out. It always screams loudest.

Yes. Fuck. Yes.

My tits. He has them.

Fuck. Yes.

They fit. His hands fit over them. Holding them in a hard grasp with his fingers, he rubs his calloused palms over both nipples.

Shiiiiiiit.

Eyes squished up tight. Muscles clenched. Fist tugging at his hair. Tongue wresting with his. My clit on his thigh, screaming. But my breasts. *Fuck.* My breasts.

He makes me explode all over his thigh and I scream.

Never. Never have I felt this. Ever. *Oh God.*

Minutes and minutes of exquisite fucking pleasure. Throbbing through me. Intense. Insane. Indulgence.

He holds me against his chest. His hands run along my spine. I can breathe again.

My body returns. Piece by piece.

His chest helps. Pressed so it crushes my boobs, but supports them, holding them tightly on well-developed pectoral muscles. His thigh, motionless between my legs, centres me. His curls in my clenched fingers give me softness. A ragged breath lets me know I'm not alone in this crushing release.

Slowly I put myself back together. It's then I notice he's rock hard. He hasn't come.

Before I can worry about that, his gentle hands spread across my shoulder blades, soothing, holding, supporting.

"Jan-ice, are you okay?"

I stretch forwards and lick along his pouty lower lip before speaking as I nibble against his mouth. "You are goddamn incredible. I've never come like that in my life."

A groan from behind makes me freeze.

Michael?

Dear God. Michael. He watched that. He's watching now.

Fuck.

Emil picks me up and curls me against his chest as if I'm a child and not a woman he's just satisfied. He sits on the edge of the bed and I burrow my face against his chest and shoulder. Mortified.

I've just come on the leg of a stranger while my husband watched.

"Don't think." Emil's mouth hovers over my ear so his words are whispered softly into my mind. Then he slowly coaxes my head up and turns it so I can see Michael. Well, I suppose I could see him if I opened my eyes. I can't. I don't think I can look at him ever again.

How could I do that to him? How could I forget he was there?

I've never had an orgasm like that in my life.

I'm—

"Look at your husband, Jan-ice." He waits but still I can't open my eyes. "You're perfectly matched. He came as you did. His come is all over the floor and all over him. Yet his cock is still hard. He's waiting for you to come again." Emil's voice slithers through my bruised mind, easing my regrets.

Did Michael really come? Watching that?

My eyes fly open.

Michael's wiping cum off his stomach and chest with a towel. His cock is still semi-hard, and that's not an easy feat. Not any more, anyway. And he's panting every bit as hard as me. His eyes are glazed there's a smile still tugging at the corner of his mouth. Michael's pleasure halts my fears.

I relax against Emil's wide chest and he doesn't need any other sign that I'm okay. That Michael is okay. That we're both going to continue.

His hands swoop beneath my breasts, lifting and presenting them to Michael.

"You were right, Michael. Jan-ice has magnificent breasts. So responsive." He flicks my left nipple and then the right, causing me to moan the first time and groan needily the second. Michael stops his cleaning and stares at us.

Emil plays with my breasts while I squirm on his lap. His cock presses hard against my buttocks, hips or thigh, whichever part skims across the middle of his lap while I wriggle. Michael can't take his eyes off us. His hands are closed around his cock and he's stroking it.

Michael's cock is not as long as Emil's, although I haven't seen them together. Actually, I haven't had a good examination of Emil's. But as it presses against me, I know it's bigger than Michael's. And it holds on longer too. Michael would never have waited so long before he fucked me. There's no way he'd do what Emil has just done. No way.

Emil lifts me to my feet and stands me in front of him facing Michael. "Would you like Michael to watch again, Jan-ice?" I can't speak but I do manage a nod.

Emil spreads my legs and kneels between them. He looks up at me. "Will you rub your tits like I would? I want to taste you." I groan and it's not feminine. It's lusty and needy. "And if you need to scream, make sure you tell your husband how good my tongue is."

With my head thrown back, I can't see Michael but I hear him. I hear his sharp intake of breath. His light groan. Then the slick movement of skin on skin. He's stroking himself.

I want to watch but before I can look, Emil has his mouth on my cunt and he sucks. I curl my hands into fists. Holding tight. Nails into flesh.

His fingers, lips and tongue all move, sending my brain into another meltdown. I don't think my legs can hold me upright. If his tongue—

Jesus.

My knees buckle and I fall onto the bed. Emil falls with me. His tongue fucks into me. Deep. Hard. Over and over again.

The suction and the intense pressure never lets up. No rest. No chance to relax. Just wave after wave of intense pressure and pleasure. Flowing over me, through me, thrilling me.

Feet hooked on the the edge of the bed, my hands slide to my breasts. Smaller than his hands. Smoother than his hands. But it doesn't matter. His tongue and mouth have me on the precipice, every cell in my body screams for release and yet I want this to last, forever.

I twist my nipples like *he* did but I can't grip hard enough or twist tight enough. All I can do is pinch and pluck. Squeeze and lift. Writhe in bliss.

"Is it good, Jan?"

Fuck. It's so fucking good.

I don't want him to stop. Ever. His mouth is... *Shit. It's Michael asking.*

I'm meant to answer. Pleasure him by telling him how I feel. I can't make words. I have to try. I have to do my part. I can't just accept all this pleasure without giving back. To Michael, not Emil. I need to focus on Michael. Michael.

I concentrate on breathing, clearing my mind of some of the lust-fog, and finding words.

"It's so fucking good." Words. I'm so proud of myself.

Emil's tongue stops against my clit. His stare meets mine.

"You have to do better than that." Emil grins

wickedly. It's unspoken but somehow I know. *Hell.* If I don't do better, he isn't going down on me again.

With wide eyes and a loud groan, I muster thoughts. I want Emil's face in my cunt.

"His hands were amazing but his tongue." I grab a breath and try to explain. "Fuck. His tongue does things —" I scream, almost leaping from the bed as his tongue thrusts inside and twists.

Things like that.

Fuck.

Emil's mouth goes away. I know he wants more words. Good words. Full sentences even. How can I talk when I can barely concentrate enough to breathe?

I focus on Michael. And his stroking hand. His cock's straining beneath his curled fingers.

So long as I concentrate on Michael and don't look at Emil, I can squeeze oxygen into my lungs.

"His tongue...God, Michael. It's like he can't eat enough of me, like he can't taste me deeply enough. Like he wants to suck me dry, drowning in my juices as he feeds." Every word is an effort and they're prised slowly from me but I keep speaking because with every sentence, Michael's face contorts further. His eyes squint as if he wants to keep my gaze but can't bear to do so either. He's twisting in the chair, like he's bound. My heart is huge in my chest, almost bursting from me. I'm hurting him even as I arouse him. "He's so good—"

Emil's fingers make me leap. They spread wide my nether lips so I'm completely exposed. I should feel uncomfortable or at least a little embarrassed but I'm not. Michael is so close to coming as Emil exposes me. The fact that Emil wants to look at me, at the very centre of me, turns me on. They'll both know it too because there's a trickle of need moving from my vagina.

There's a moan like someone's hurting and it's not from me.

Goddamn. Fuck. God.

I scream the words out loud. I thought it was in my head.

There's a strangled sound that becomes, "What? Tell me."

"Tongue inside. Lapping."

Fuck.

"Thumb on my arse."

He's pressing both my openings and I'm going to fucking explode.

"Shit." Loud panting. It's me. Adjusting. "Arse. Two. Inside. Moving." I hope to God Michael can work that out. Words aren't easily found at the moment. My brain is filled with the most intense pleas—

"Jesuuuuuuuuuuus."

Michael's eyes are wide, his hand's beating fast. He's almost ready to come and so am—

There's a goddamn pause in the movement of Emil's fingers. *Words.* I need fucking words.

"Emil is a fucking sex god and I don't want him to leave."

Fuck.

I scream those words. At Michael.

I squeeze my eyes closed imagining the horror Michael's experiencing from my betrayal. But then there's panting, gasping, little noises like someone's about ready to come. I prise my eyelids apart. *Dear God.* I blink. Quickly.

Michael.

He's beating his cock so fast his hand's a blur. Legs spread wide, his balls are tucked up tight against his body. His cock jerks. Precum makes his cockhead slick, glistening in the light.

As I stare, air fills my body in bursts.

I can't suck in enough. I'm tingling. Everywhere.

Emil lashes my clit with his tongue while his fingers stretch my body. Pulsing waves of pleasure wash through me. Again.

Orgasm central.

Shuddering tremors tear me.

Emil's hands stroke, tease, not letting me ride out my pleasure. Before I can speak, he lifts my legs. The backs of my thighs meet flesh, hot and tight. I prise my eyelids open and Emil looms over me. His hands hold my legs up against his chest. My calves frame his gorgeous head.

"You're so beautiful." I'm staring at Emil's cock which is a huge throbbing mass of need but behind him there's the tortured face of my husband. I don't know who is more beautiful but it doesn't matter. Michael hears me say it to Emil and he's aghast but so fucking aroused. I've never seen him look like that. He can't stop staring at the gap between Emil's cock and my cunt. His hot gaze darts across the space. Back and forth. Back and forth. He wants to close the gap.

I want that too. "Fuck me. Please." I stare into his eyes and they stare back.

"Why do you want my cock, Jan-ice? You've had plenty of pleasure already, surely?"

God. He's going to make me say it.

I look at Michael again. He's desperately staring. Mouth open. He meets my gaze, silently begging me to speak. He wants Emil to fuck me.

I close my eyes tight. Draw in air.

I'll do anything for Michael. I want him filled with pleasure, through my pleasure. Even if it's with another man.

I bite my lips.

I have to humiliate him further to give him the release he needs.

Oh, Michael.

I turn my gaze to Emil. "Your cock is the biggest I've ever seen. I want to feel it. Inside me."

A gasp from my husband makes me turn my head. The pain on his face almost stalls the rest of my words, but the clench of his hand on his cock and the mad stroking shows how much he wants this, even as it batters him.

I focus on Emil again. He holds still, as if waiting for the right words to pass my lips. "I want to be stretched wide. I want to know what that big cock feels like. What I've missed."

Another hiss of hurt and I worry that I've gone too far.

I look at my husband and his hand is beating an even faster rhythm so I continue to deal out pain. "Emil's mouth and fingers are the best I've ever felt. He clearly loves sex. I want to know what it's like to be fucked by someone who loves fucking. I don't want duty, or usual, or every day. I want spectacular. I know he can give me what you can't."

God. I hate myself.

When I look at Michael, he's not only beating off hard but he's crying. The sheen on his cheeks has to be tears.

Fucking idiot.

I've no idea if I'm cursing myself or him. Have I gone too far? But he wants humiliation. He told me to say this but will he hate me?

Emil slides on a condom before his cock enters me in one movement. Filling me. Stopping my brain. The world is reduced to the sharp pain of my flesh stretching. Michael blurs as my eyes fill.

So thick.

So strong.

Maybe I said those words because Michael's gaze darkens, his lips part, he's sucking in deep breaths.

Emil moves and I'm caught by the rhythm of his hips against mine.

Emil nuzzles beside my ear. "What does it feel like now?"

"Good." I'm stretched enough so the remnant of hurt buzzes against the pleasure.

Emil nudges me.

"Great." I manage to say. Then I upgrade it. "Amazing." I'm adjusting to his size.

He licks my earlobe. "Louder." He hesitates while his words penetrate my lust. "Or I stop."

Crap.

Maybe I haven't been voicing all this to Michael. Maybe it's just my gaze that's arousing him, or the sight of me impaled on this big cock.

I have to find words between this....bliss?

When Emil's rhythmic thrusts halt, words come.

"He's so big." I'm proud I've managed to breathe out a few words. Loudly. Michael hears and nods. I need to focus on Michael so I can arouse, and hurt him, in order to get my orgasm.

Emil thrusts. Once.

"Hard." No movement. "He's so hard. Harder than you, Michael. Bigger than you."

The thrusts come with each phrase so that a rhythm marks the beat of my words. When the words stop, that hard cock withdraws so only the tip is inside me.

"Tight. I'm so fucking tight." The last word comes out as a squeal when that big cock thrusts inside me again. I keep up the words. A patter of hard, big, thick, tight. Stupid words. Words that keep that big cock filling me, stretching me, taking me closer to the perfect oblivion.

My muscles clench around his cock as he rocks into and out of me. I'm staring at my husband, watching his pleasure as my own expands. "This is what I want. This is perfect. It's so fucking perfect."

Michael's groan almost kills me, but Emil distracts me in the best way possible, fucking me so hard I can't think. In, out, in out. Faster and harder than I thought I could take.

I can't drop Michael's gaze. Our connection can't be

broken even as I'm fucked more thoroughly than ever before.

It's wave upon wave of pleasure. For me. For Michael.

I arch and scream, which sends Michael over the edge. A white stream of cum shoots from him as his hand works like a piston around his jetting cock. I can hardly focus on that majestic sight or Michael's orgasmic face as my own release screams through. My eyes lose focus, my brain function shatters, and my body takes flight.

I think I'm going to die. From coming.

After the longest orgasm of my life, where my body became nothing but a bundle of rippling termors, I'm soothed and petted. Bundled into strong arms and cradled to sleep.

When I wake, I'm incredibly sore but tingling with newfound arousal.

Fingers stroke along my spine and I arch, tipping my head backwards where it rests on a strong shoulder. Lips nuzzle my neck, my ear, my jaw. They move as I do, until we're kissing, long and deep and right.

His cock is hard against my buttocks and I rub against it.

So right.

So perfect.

My mouth pulls from his and I whisper, "Take me, please." I'm begging and I don't care. I want his cock inside me.

"You're sore."

"You'll be gentle." I know he will.

I roll towards him. Michael. My lover. Husband.

Hero.

I stroke his cheek as our gazes lock. His cock slides into me. Arching from the bed into him, I close my eyes briefly as the sensation washes across me.

"Michael. You're perfect."

He groans and I feel it rumble against my stomach and chest before it's exhaled.

His hips rock into me, his cock strong and powerful but gentle against my tender flesh.

"Yes," I moan. "Like that."

His sliding is just what I need. Slow, not too deep but deep enough to arouse.

One hand holds my hip, the other teases my breast. Gently.

Then he licks across my bruised nipples and I clench.

"Michael." It's a gasp of pure bliss.

His body knows mine. Knows what I want. What I need. And gives it to me.

He knows what I want. What I need. And gives it to me.

I have the best husband in the world.

"I love you, Michael."

Our lips meet as a gentle morning orgasm slips over us, taking us to our heaven.

The room is empty except for us. Emil is just another fantasy. Over.

Michael is my reality.

The End

~

ABOUT THE AUTHOR

Cate Ellink became intrigued by the erotic when her grandfather used to pass books to her father saying, "Don't let the girls read page X." Although her mother and sisters never bothered to chase those pages, Cate always did. Invariably, her imagination was better than what she read. While pursuing a career in science, Cate amused herself by writing about ordinary events and giving them an erotic twist. It's taken more than a few years to bravely expose her mind to the public. While the events in her stories may have occurred, it's highly likely that her imagination is far more exciting than the reality. Cate lives near the beach in NSW with a long-suffering husband.

Find Cate on:
Website: http://www.cateellink.com
Email: cate@cateellink.com

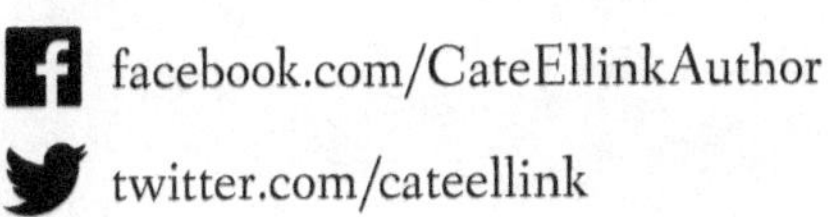
facebook.com/CateEllinkAuthor

twitter.com/cateellink